Praise for
The Magical Worlds of The Lord of the Rings

"[Colbert has written] readers' guides that actually help broaden readers' perspectives on where certain mega-selling fantasy works come from...What Colbert does rather well with Harry Potter and now Tolkien is to take aspects of the respective books and ponder their likely origins...In short chapters and easy-to-read language, this is an ideal stocking stuffer for Tolkien fans."
—*The Toronto Star*

"It can be read by audiences whose level of familiarity with Tolkien will range from the new initiate to the college students who started the 'Frodo Lives' campaign. Considering the book is classified alphabetically by subject, the flow from one section to the next makes it a pleasant read from cover to cover and the bibliography is useful for those inspired to read further. A good companion for those reading the books for the first time, it is more helpful than the drier, highly academic reference books on Tolkien that appeal to the scholar or seriously devoted fan. The page design with its fascinating fact sidebars has the feel of a textbook, but without the mandatory purgatory associations of school. It is also a highly useful behind-the-pages look at Tolkien's sources and inspirations and an introduction for those who have seen the movies and want to know a bit more."
—*SFRevu*

"Tolkien's epic fantasies deserve a strong readers' supplement, and David Colbert's *The Magical Worlds of The Lord of the Rings* will appeal to any[one] interested in the folklore and legends behind his Middle-earth worlds. From Finnish sagas to Shakespeare and King Arthur, *The Magical Worlds of The Lord of the Rings* draws together insights from other works of fiction and fable to lend added depth to Tolkien's creation."
—*Midwest Book Review*

"An exploration of the ancient myths and legends as well as more recent history that inspired J.R.R. Tolkien, and sparked his incredible imagination...The book explains the inner concepts of Tolkien's book and the timeless, universal theme of good vs. evil. Explained in fascinating detail is why Tolkien wanted to create an entire mythology that would rival those of ancient cultures such as Greece and Rome. Written for longtime fans of the books as well as more recent fans who know Middle-earth from the silver screen...a complex and satisfying read." —*The Nation* (Thailand)

"Highly dip-inable. It's not exhaustive, neither is it elitist academically, and will serve as a good introduction for young readers to the long histories of myth, legends, and literature." —*The New Zealand Herald*

"From Bilbo Baggins to Saruman, Colbert goes through Tolkien's work with a fine-toothed comb trying to find inspirations for the many characters, places and themes of Middle-earth. By analyzing the great epochs in the life of Tolkien and their relation to his writings, Colbert shows the true earthly soul of *The Lord of the Rings* and defines its place in the written history of England. Although the book never goes so deep as to destroy the magic of Tolkien, its analysis is thorough enough to keep the reader interested from page to page, while still leaving the mystery that attracts such a huge Tolkien fan base...definitely recommended as a stepping stone toward further reading into Tolkien after *The Lord of the Rings* or just as an interesting read for the Tolkien novice." —*The Advertiser*

"Even the would-be Tolkien scholar and hardcore fan with well-worn and half-memorized copies of all the books in the series will find this volume interesting. The index, bibliography and glossary make for handy entrances to the book...The inspiration from Tolkien's knowledge of ancient English and North European lore is well-trodden ground for the initiated, but Colbert presents it in an easy-to-read manner with plenty of line drawings that will be entertaining for any reader, whether they just saw the movie or can quote Gandalf chapter and verse." —Rambles.net

Praise for
The Magical Worlds of Harry Potter

"Digs deep into different cultures and mythologies to piece together the origins of Rowling's characters. Learn about griffins, goblins, Latin and why Harry is a universal hero." —*The Baltimore Sun*

"A feast for future game-show contestants...You could use it as reference to set up a round of *Jeopardy!*" —*Orlando Sentinel*

"A guide to the history, literature and mythology Rowling sprinkles throughout...Grown-ups might like [it] too, because it painlessly exposes youngsters to Shakespeare, Chaucer, Ovid, Flaubert and more. Fun to read." —*St. Louis Post-Dispatch*

"This irresistibly dippable book gently draws children into the joys of works of reference. A glorious tribute to Rowling's work." —*The Times* (London)

"[An] enthusiast's treasury of facts." —*The Times Educational Supplement*

"David Colbert gives a fresh insight into Rowling's books." —*New Straits Times* (Malaysia)

"All the questions you wanted to ask about the magical world of Harry Potter are answered here. Colbert explains the origins of magical creatures, the clues to hidden meanings in names, and amazing facts about real-life wizards and ancient magic spells...In essence, this book decodes her clues to reveal the artfully hidden meanings. Excellent." —*The Nation* (Thailand)

"*The Magical Worlds of Harry Potter* might just be the trivia to appease Potter fans...Colbert's work is at its best when delving into the historic basis behind characters, creatures and magical lore... Mythological and legendary creatures enjoyed featured roles in the Potter stories, and Colbert details the legends behind the legends in brief, easily digested snippets. The carefully chosen art, frequently wood-block carvings or etchings from Egyptian antiquities, adds a fascinating realistic element to his explanations...[This book] provides delightful companion pieces for the currently available novels. And best of all, it might inspire young readers to learn Latin, research a wizard or witch from historical times, or pen their own epic hero to send on a magical quest." —Rambles.net

Titles by David Colbert

The Magical Worlds of Philip Pullman
The Magical Worlds of Narnia
The Magical Worlds of The Lord of the Rings
The Magical Worlds of Harry Potter

The Hidden Myths in Harry Potter: Spellbinding Map and Book of Secrets

Eyewitness to America
Eyewitness to the American West
Eyewitness to Wall Street

WWII: A Tribute in Art and Literature
Baseball: A Celebration in Art and Literature

THE MAGICAL WORLDS OF PHILIP PULLMAN

A TREASURY OF FASCINATING FACTS

DAVID COLBERT

BERKLEY BOOKS, NEW YORK

THE BERKLEY PUBLISHING GROUP
Published by the Penguin Group
Penguin Group (USA) Inc.
375 Hudson Street, New York, New York 10014, USA
Penguin Group (Canada), 90 Eglinton Avenue East, Suite 700, Toronto, Ontario M4P 2Y3, Canada
(a division of Pearson Penguin Canada Inc.)
Penguin Books Ltd., 80 Strand, London WC2R 0RL, England
Penguin Group Ireland, 25 St. Stephen's Green, Dublin 2, Ireland (a division of Penguin Books Ltd.)
Penguin Group (Australia), 250 Camberwell Road, Camberwell, Victoria 3124, Australia
(a division of Pearson Australia Group Pty. Ltd.)
Penguin Books India Pvt. Ltd., 11 Community Centre, Panchsheel Park, New Delhi—110 017, India
Penguin Group (NZ), Cnr. Airborne and Rosedale Roads, Albany, Auckland 1310, New Zealand
(a division of Pearson New Zealand Ltd.)
Penguin Books (South Africa) (Pty.) Ltd., 24 Sturdee Avenue, Rosebank, Johannesburg 2196,
South Africa

Penguin Books Ltd., Registered Offices: 80 Strand, London WC2R 0RL, England

This book is an original publication of The Berkley Publishing Group.

This book was not authorized, prepared, approved, licensed, or endorsed by Random House, Inc., New Line Cinema, or any other individual or entity associated with the HIS DARK MATERIALS books or any movies based on those books.

The publisher does not have any control over and does not assume responsibility for third-party websites or their content.

PRINTING HISTORY
Berkley trade paperback edition / April 2006

Library of Congress Cataloging-in-Publication Data

Colbert, David.
 The magical worlds of Philip Pullman : a treasury of fascinating facts / by David Colbert.
  p. cm.
 Includes bibliographical references.
 ISBN 0-425-20790-0
  1. Pullman, Philip, 1946– His dark materials. 2. Young adult fiction, English—History and criticism. 3. Fantasy fiction, English—History and criticism. I. Title.

PR6066.U44Z58 2006
823'.914—dc22

2005044877

PRINTED IN THE UNITED STATES OF AMERICA

10 9 8 7 6 5 4 3 2 1

With thanks to
Leona Nevler,
John Morgan,
Lara Robbins
and Philip Pullman
for their generous assistance

MISS PRISM: Memory, my dear Cecily, is the diary that we all carry about with us.

CECILY: Yes, but it usually chronicles the things that have never happened, and couldn't possibly have happened. I believe that Memory is responsible for nearly all the three-volume novels that Mudie sends us.

MISS PRISM: Do not speak slightingly of the three-volume novel, Cecily. I wrote one myself in earlier days.

CECILY: Did you really, Miss Prism? How wonderfully clever you are! I hope it did not end happily? I don't like novels that end happily. They depress me so much.

MISS PRISM: The good ended happily, and the bad unhappily. That is what Fiction means.

Oscar Wilde, *The Importance of Being Earnest*

contents

Introduction   1

What Does the Trilogy Owe to *Paradise Lost*?   5
    On Milton's Blindness   8
    Diamond Life   18

How Did William Blake Influence Lyra's Story?   27
    "A Grain of Sand in Lambeth That Satan Cannot Find"   30
    Lyra Belacqua: Little Girl Lost   38
    "The Girl for Me"   41
    See No Evil: Specters in Pullman and Blake   44

What Makes Iorek Byrnison So Smart?   49

Is Lord Asriel the Story's Hero?   57
    Body Double   62
    You Little Devil   70

Does Mrs. Coulter Really Change?   75
    Monkeyshines   78

How New Are Pullman's Ideas?   85
   Where Angels Fear to Tread   88

Who Gave Daemons to Humankind?   97
   The Pantalaimon Code   102
   Plenty of Moxie   105
   I Need That Like I Need a Hole in the Head   110

Who Tried to Invent a Real Alethiometer?   113
   Positively Negative   116

How Shall Death Die?   129
   Blake's Illustrations for Dante's Divine Comedy 134
   "America: A Prophecy"   137

Bibliography and Notes   147

INTRODUCTION

After asking me to write this book, my British publishers, who have published Philip Pullman, said they'd written to him as a courtesy to tell him about the project. His response was revealing. More than just agreeing to answer questions, he volunteered that he wouldn't try to influence my conclusions. That's not a common reaction. People who are about to be the subject of a book are usually wary, and want to influence what's written. Pullman would have even more reason to be concerned, because his views on religion have attracted many hostile critics. His ideas have often been described inaccurately, and twisted to make them easier to oppose. Yet Pullman remains open to discussion and debate.

The reason is more than a desire to talk about his work. Most of the time he'd rather let his books stand on their own with no commentary. He simply remains curious about the larger questions that first led him to write *His Dark Materials*. He's not done thinking about life and the afterlife, about

God and sin and organized religion. Along with that curiosity is a belief that intellectual honesty requires an open mind. Many of Pullman's critics attack him for denouncing C. S. Lewis, the author of the Christian-influenced *Chronicles of Narnia*, without realizing Pullman's anger is largely a reaction to Lewis's intellectual style. Even Lewis's friends admitted he usually started his essays or books by assuming he knew all the answers, and then would make up weak questions for the opposite side of the argument. That's the reverse of what Pullman does. Pullman's first concern is the quality of the questions.

Before I understood this, there were some interesting exchanges. If you've read any of my other Magical Worlds books, you know that I like strange details as much as larger themes. In some cases they're interesting clues. The books of J. R. R. Tolkien, for example, are filled with names invented from the ancient languages Tolkien studied. They were one of Tolkien's ways of understanding and creating the imaginary history of Middle-earth. Because I didn't want to ask Pullman the same questions he's been asked in nearly every interview—things like, "What would *your* daemon be?"—the first questions I asked were about some of the small details I'd noticed. Thinking I was simply easing into the process, I asked him why the character Mary Malone mentions marzipan, an almond-paste candy, in a scene that's meant as a parallel to the serpent's offer of an apple to Eve in Genesis. I wondered if maybe Pullman had something specific in mind when he chose that unusual treat. Could it refer to a piece of scripture? It's the kind of detail other authors use to reveal an interesting facet of the story. And when you're looking at a desk full of notes, sometimes it's the small, odd one that stands out first.

Pullman wasn't happy with that question. With all the bigger issues the book raises, he wondered, why was I looking at this insignificant detail? Though he didn't say it, his message was clear. He didn't mind if my book argued fiercely against his views, but he did mind if I wasn't going to start with the right questions.

That wasn't the last oddball question I asked, but from then on I explained my thinking first. Fortunately, I wasn't interested in digging up all the small allusions he planted in this story. They're clues to what he was reading, and therefore to steps in his thinking, but they don't add up to an understanding of the major themes. He bends nearly every allusion to fit the shape of his own ideas.

His Dark Materials can be read as a storehouse of Pullman's own questions. What happens after death? Is God really like the Bible describes? Why do some people claim to have a unique insight into God? Why do good intentions sometimes lead to terrible consequences, and wicked plans sometimes lead to benefits for humankind? It's in Pullman's nature to examine these questions with a combination of intellectual honesty and rigor. He tries to ask the right questions; and, much more rare, he makes an effort to remain open to any answer, regardless of how it fits into his existing beliefs.

Pullman's questions have led him to conclusions that many people find difficult to face. He sees a world without God or heaven or an eternal afterlife. He often doesn't see clear boundaries between right and wrong. It's a messy and uncertain adult world. At the same time, it's full of moral choices and serious consequences.

It's also a world that's focused on spiritual meaning. Nicholas Hynter, who directed a theatrical adaptation of *His Dark Materials* for the National Theatre in London, explains his view of it: "The thing about these books is that they take our metaphyical needs very seriously. They are not impressed by certain aspects of organized religion, but what they are steeped in is the need to find stories and symbols which explain to us the numinous, that which is beyond our understanding. In other words, it seems to me that the impulse behind these books is very close to a religious impulse."

I agree. Pullman says he's an atheist and that we must make the most of life in our material world, but in *His Dark Materials* the question of how to achieve spiritual fulfillment is always centerstage.

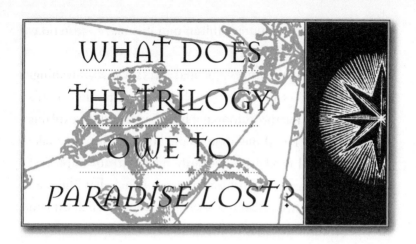

WHAT DOES THE TRILOGY OWE TO PARADISE LOST?

For readers eager to learn more about *His Dark Materials*, there's good news and bad news. The good news: Pullman has revealed his original inspiration was John Milton's epic poem *Paradise Lost*. The bad news: Pullman has revealed his original inspiration was John Milton's epic poem *Paradise Lost*.

People talk about that poem as if it's the Mount Everest of English class—mammoth, spotted with the corpses of people who didn't survive the climb, and conquerable only if an expert drags you to the summit with a rope.

That reputation is an exaggeration. First, *Paradise Lost* isn't any longer than a normal novel. At about eighty thousand words, it's shorter than the shortest volume of Pullman's trilogy, *The Subtle Knife*, which contains about

John Milton
(1608–1674)

How strong was
Milton's distaste
for arbitrary
authority? Two
weeks after the
execution of
King Charles I in
January 1649,
Milton published
a pamphlet
defending the
execution.
"No sacrifice
to God," he
wrote, is "more
acceptable than
an unjust and
wicked king."
Milton objected
to Charles's
method of ruling
as an absolute
monarch without
deference to
Parliament.

a hundred thousand. Nor is *Paradise Lost* uphill all the way. It's not a boring sermon about sin, as many expect. It's a story about an ambitious villain, a cunning plan to rule the world, and a great battle to settle the fate of humankind.

Milton himself may surprise you too. Though one expert has joked that Milton is the "deadest" of the dead poets that students hate to study, Milton was actually a rebel, passionate about liberty in an age when there was little of it. Milton wrote a strong argument for freedom of the press at a time when demanding it was a courageous act. He challenged the hierarchy of bishops that ruled the Church of England even after the Protestant Reformation, calling for greater democracy in the church. During the English Civil Wars (1642–1645 and 1648–1649), he supported the overthrow of the monarchy. He held a high post in the government of Oliver Cromwell, leader of the temporarily successful rebellion, who as Lord Protector was the only civilian head of state in Britain's history. After the monarchy was restored, Milton was almost executed for defying the authority of the king and the church. His masterpiece reflects this rebellious spirit.

If you're inclined to read *Paradise Lost*,

you'll come across familiar passages. Pullman has borrowed various elements from the epic, including his trilogy's title. (More about that in a moment.) But reading *Paradise Lost* isn't a requirement for understanding *His Dark Materials*. And though it can be fun to find allusions to it in *His Dark Materials*, they don't add up to a secret decoder book. What's interesting is the general influence of Milton on Pullman, and the way *His Dark Materials* fits into centuries of literature and art inspired by *Paradise Lost*.

AN APPLE A DAY

The basic plot of *Paradise Lost* is easy to understand. It comes from the Old Testament story of Adam and Eve. Milton gets right to the point in the opening lines:

> *Of Man's first disobedience, and the fruit*
> *Of that forbidden tree whose mortal taste*
> *Brought death into the World, and all our*
> *   woe,*
> *With loss of Eden, till one greater Man*
> *Restore us, and regain the blissful seat,*
> *Sing, Heavenly Muse . . .*

In Milton's version, the story begins when Satan, having been exiled from Heaven for

The muse Milton invokes in the poem's first lines is Urania, whom the Romans considered the muse of astronomy. Her name means "heavenly one." Poets of the Renaissance adopted her as the muse of Christian poetry.

On Milton's Blindness

The first thing people learn about Milton's personal life is that he was blind. That's only part of the story. He went blind as an adult. He was 43 when his blindness became complete. To continue writing, he dictated to secretaries, including the poet Andrew Marvell.

Paradise Lost is among the works Milton dictated. Some critics have made a lot of this fact. The poet T. S. Eliot, who sidelined in criticism, believed that Milton's blindness led to a lack of visual imagery in *Paradise Lost*. That's not one of Eliot's strongest theories.

There's plenty of imagery in *Paradise Lost*. Also, many other writers, especially those with a political and intellectual nature like Milton's, pay less attention to imagery than Eliot did.

Milton wrote a sonnet about his condition, Sonnet XIX, often referred to as "On His Blindness," that's counted among the best in literature. The last line has become so commonplace it's often mistaken as a quotation from the Bible.

Sonnet XIX

When I consider how my light is spent
    Ere half my days in this dark world and wide,
    And that one talent which is death to hide
    Lodged with me useless, though my soul more bent
To serve therewith my maker, and present
    My true account, lest he returning, chide,
    "Doth God exact day-labour, light denied?"
    I fondly ask. But Patience, to prevent
That murmur, soon replies, "God doth not need
    Either man's work or his own gifts; who best
    Bear his mild yoke, they serve him best; his state
Is kingly. Thousands at his bidding speed,
    And post o'er land and ocean without rest;
    They also serve who only stand and wait."

defying God, sits with his underlings around a lake of fire and plans his revenge. He gathers demons to defeat God's angels. He tempts Adam and Eve to disobey God by eating fruit from the Tree of Forbidden Knowledge. They do, and curse humankind with sin. But then God shows humankind there's a way to free itself of sin: faith in his Son.

Some similarities with *His Dark Materials* are revealed even in that short summary. Soon after Pullman's story begins, Lord Asriel is in prison. He schemes to gather an army to fight the Authority. Lyra and Will are tempted to "sin," as the Magisterium would put it, by Mary Malone.

Important differences also appear. In *His Dark Materials*, Lyra and Will are right to defy the Authority and the Magisterium. They don't curse humankind with sin. They save an infinite number of worlds.

This is why Pullman often explains he decided to recast Milton's story by "reversing the moral polarities."

THE DEVIL'S PARTY

Though that reversal may sound like a modern idea, Milton was accused of doing something similar. In his case, it was said that *Paradise Lost* inverted the morality of the Bible. As

The word "pandemonium," which in modern English means a place of chaos, was coined by Milton for *Paradise Lost*. Milton used it as the name of the place where demons live. *Pan* is the ancient Greek word for "all."

soon as *Paradise Lost* was published in 1667, readers noticed Milton devotes a lot of the work to explaining Satan's psyche, and does such a good job of it that many readers are tempted by Satan's arguments for tasting the forbidden fruit.

An example is how reasonable Satan seems when he explains why he thinks Adam and Eve should taste the forbidden fruit of knowledge:

> *Knowledge forbidden?*
> [That's] *Suspicious, reasonless. Why should*
>   *their Lord*
> *Envy them that? Can it be sin to know?*
> *Can it be death? And do they only stand*
> *By ignorance? Is that their happy state,*
> *The proof of their obedience and their*
>   *faith?*
> (*Paradise Lost*, Book II, lines 515–520)

Paradise Lost first appeared in 1667. A few years later Milton revised it to divide it into twelve long sections, following the form of Virgil's *Aeneid.*

Satan is saying faith based on ignorance is weak. It makes a mockery of devotion to God. Obedience and devotion should be choices.

Another example: Satan's plan to tempt Adam and Eve isn't entirely selfish. It's not just a way to overthrow God. He sincerely believes it will free Adam and Eve from unfair constraints:

Hence I will excite their minds
With more desire to know, and to reject
Envious commands, invented with design
To keep them low . . .
(*Paradise Lost*, Book IV, lines 522–525)

After the Restoration of the British monarchy in 1660, Milton, like many supporters of Cromwell's Commonwealth, went into hiding. He was captured, but released as part of a general amnesty of rebels.

Milton's Satan believes God is keeping human-kind in ignorance because it serves God's ego. It almost seems as if God is the selfish one. That perspective is similar to Pullman's. Readers of *His Dark Materials* who cringe when members of the Magisterium are patronizing to Lyra will recognize the same tone from the authority figures in *Paradise Lost*. After Adam asks some questions about the universe, the archangel Michael replies,

Heaven is for thee too high
To know what passes there; be lowly wise;
Think only what concerns thee and thy
*   being;*
Dream not of other worlds . . .
(*Paradise Lost*, Book VIII, lines 172–175)

Shouldn't God be flattered by Adam's interest, instead of frightened by Adam's curiosity? Isn't Adam's desire to understand God's world of wonders a form of devotion? True, it might

THE TEMPTATION OF EVE

So saying, her rash hand in evil hour
Forth-reaching to the fruit, she plucked, she eat

"The Temptation of Eve," from William Blake's
illustrations to *Paradise Lost* (1808)

take Michael a long time to explain the universe, but Adam has time. He's immortal.

In his famous pamphlet defending free speech, Milton used Adam as an example:
"When God gave [Adam] reason, he gave him freedom to choose, for reason is but choosing; he had else been a mere artificial Adam. . . . God therefore left him free."
—from *Areopagitica: a Speech for the Liberty of Unlicensed* [Uncensored] *Printing* (1644)

A bit more than a century after the epic was written, the poet William Blake (1757–1827) wrote something that Pullman quotes often: Blake said Milton was "of the Devil's party without knowing it." Blake meant that even though Milton begins *Paradise Lost* by saying the poem will "justify the ways of God," Milton does a better job of arguing against those ways. He makes God's demand for obedience seem petty. He makes the hunger for knowledge seem admirable.

Blake said Milton showed sympathy for the devil because Milton was "a true poet." Blake meant Milton was naturally on the side of passion and rebellion and personal freedom. Oxford University professor A. B. Nuttall offers the observation that all the Milton scholars since Blake can be roughly divided into those who believe *Paradise Lost* follows Christian teaching and those who, like Blake, "detected unorthodox energies everywhere."

Pullman believes Blake was right. He says writing *His Dark Materials* meant "doing consciously what Blake said Milton did without knowing it, and telling the story from the devil's point of view."

As Pullman puts it, *Paradise Lost* has "the power of suggesting all kinds of correspondences and echoes." You can hear them throughout *His Dark Materials*, sometimes faintly, sometimes clearly.

Start at the beginning: The phrase "His Dark Materials" comes from Milton's poem. You may have noticed the lines Pullman quotes at the beginning of the trilogy's first volume:

> *Into this wild abyss,*
> *The womb of nature, and perhaps her*
> *grave,*
> *Of neither sea, nor shore, nor air, nor fire,*
> *But all these in their pregnant causes mixed*
> *Confusedly, and which thus must ever*
> *fight,*
> *Unless the almighty maker them ordain*
> *His dark materials to create more worlds,*
> *Into this wild abyss the wary fiend*
> *Stood on the brink of hell and looked a*
> *while,*
> *Pondering his voyage . . .*
> (*Paradise Lost*, Book II, lines 910–919)

It was Milton's ambition, as early as age sixteen, to write the first truly British epic. The subjects he considered over the years included the legends of King Arthur, and the real-life resistance to the monarchy during the English Civil Wars. The subject of *Paradise Lost* had originally come to mind for something else entirely: a verse play.

In this passage, Satan looks at what seems to be a vast, dark ocean he must cross. It's the

The name "Paradise" comes from an old Iranian language, Avestan. It refers only to the enclosing (*pairi*) wall (*daeza*) around a garden. A Greek soldier who wrote about a war in Persia mistakenly used the word to refer to the garden itself, so the word entered Greek with that meaning. When the Hebrew Bible was translated into Greek in the third century B.C., the Garden of Eden became *paradeisos*.

dark emptiness between Hell, where he has been imprisoned, and Heaven. God hasn't created Earth yet—no "sea, nor shore, nor air, nor fire." The abyss is filled just with "His dark materials," the elements God combines to create life. These elements "mix confusedly" until God creates the world from them.

This passage is a perfect example of the complex connections between *Paradise Lost* and Pullman's trilogy. Pullman didn't imagine having Dust in his story because he'd read this passage in Milton. His idea about Dust came first. He found the passage when he was looking for a title that conveyed the idea of it. He was thinking of the scientific term for it in our world, "dark matter," which is the term Mary Malone uses.

In many ways the phrase "His dark materials" is a good fit. It has a nice sound, which to Pullman is important. It's evocative of something vague but significant, giving the title a wondrous quality without revealing too much. And it describes something from which life is created.

But in Pullman's story, Dust is different from Milton's "dark materials." To begin with, it's not "His." It's not God's. As the angel Xaphania says, "Conscious beings make Dust—they renew it all the time, by thinking and feeling and reflecting, by gaining wisdom and passing it on." (*The Amber Spyglass*, 491) The angel Balthamos explains, "Matter loves matter. It seeks to know more about itself, and Dust is formed. The first angels condensed out of Dust. . . ." (*The Amber Spyglass*, 31–32) In Pullman's world, the Christian God didn't use Dust to make the world; he himself was created *from* Dust. He was the first angel to be formed from it, and then lied and told the others he had created them. In truth they'd "condensed" from it as he did.

As well, in Pullman's world, the church doesn't respect Dust as the element from which the world is made. It fears Dust, because Dust represents wisdom and consciousness, which was forbidden to Adam and Eve and thus to all humans. To the Magisterium, Dust is Original Sin.

Pullman took what he wanted from the phrase and left the rest.

The word "Miltonist," now used to describe university professors who specialize in studying Milton, was coined in the 1800s to describe people who supported the right of divorce even when the church disapproved.

TRUE NORTH

Another title inspired by Milton appears on the American edition of the trilogy's first volume, *The Golden Compass*.

The title began as a plural: *The Golden Compasses*. That was Pullman's working title for the story, before he thought of *His Dark*

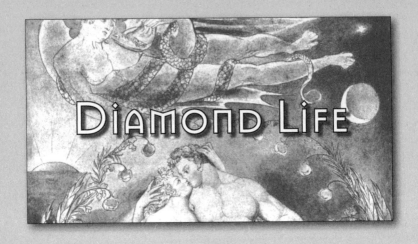

DIAMOND LIFE

Among the echoes of Milton in *His Dark Materials* are the descriptions of Lord Asriel's fortress. In *The Amber Spyglass*, Baruch sees:

> "A lake of molten sulphur extended the length of an immense canyon, releasing its mephitic vapors in sudden gusts and belches. . . . On the highest rampart of the fortress was a tower of adamant . . ."
> (*The Amber Spyglass*, 55, 57)

In *Paradise Lost*, Satan and Hell are associated with "sulphurous fire" (Book XI, line 658), "ever-burning sulphur" (Book I, line 69), "sulphur and strange fire" (Book II, line 69), and "sulphurous hail" (Book I, line 171). Pullman's word "mephitic"—meaning poisonous and stinking like burning sulphur—refers to another name for Satan, Mephistopheles.

"Adamant," the name of a crystal once considered unbreakable, is connected to Satan throughout *Paradise Lost*. Satan is imprisoned in "adamantine chains" (Book I, line 48); Hell itself has "gates of burning adamant" (Book II, line 436), "three [gates] of adamantine rock, impenetrable, impaled with circling fire" (Book II, line 646); Satan is "armed in adamant and gold" (Book VI, 277).

Why the playful borrowings? In a speech at the opening of an exhibition of illustrations for *Paradise Lost*, Pullman noted that the artists had all been inspired by "the great figure of Satan, and his quest, and its setting." He had felt the same thing, he explained. "It was . . . the visual splendor of the infernal landscapes that Milton describes . . . that inspired me in particular when, several years ago now, I was talking to my publisher about what I might write next. . . ."

That visual splendor, he has said, is what inspired him to become a writer in the first place. It happened when he read these lines of *Paradise Lost* in high school:

> *High on a Throne of Royal*
>   *State, which far*
> *Outshone the Wealth of*
>   *Ormus and of Ind,*
> *Or where the gorgeous East*
>   *with richest hand*
> *Showrs on her Kings Barbaric*
>   *Pearl and Gold,*
> *Satan exalted sat.*

"I can recall the same physical thrill I felt then," he says. "And it is physical: my skin bristles; my hair stirs; my heart beats faster."

Satan's palace: *"High on a Throne of Royal State, which far Outshone the Wealth of Ormus and of Ind."* From Gustav Doré's illustrations for *Paradise Lost* (1867)

Materials. It referred to circle-drawing compasses, not the kind that shows North, South, East, and West. The compasses are mentioned in *Paradise Lost* when God marks a design for the world:

> *He took the golden compasses, prepared*
> *In God's eternal store, to circumscribe*
> *This universe, and all created things.*
> *One foot he centred, and the other turned*
> *Round through the vast profundity obscure;*
> *And said, "'Thus far extend, thus far thy*
>   *bounds,*
> *This be thy just circumference, O World!"*
> *Thus God the Heaven created, thus the Earth,*
> *Matter unformed and void: Darkness pro-*
>   *found*
> *Covered the Abyss: but on the watery calm*
> *His brooding wings the Spirit of God out-*
>   *spread . . .*
>   *"Let there be Light!" said God . . .*
> (*Paradise Lost*, Book VII, lines 225–243)

Then someone at Pullman's American publisher assumed—"mistakenly, but firmly," as Pullman puts it—that Pullman meant the title as a reference to Lyra's alethiometer. It's round, it has pointers, and in a sense it tells Lyra the right way to go, all of which makes it

A passage in the New Testament suggests a similar image: "When he prepared the heavens, I was there: when he set a compass upon the face of the depth: when he established the clouds above: when he strengthened the fountains of the deep . . ." (Proverbs 8:27–8)

20

like the kind of compass—singular—that tells directions. By the time Pullman had found the title he wanted to use, *Northern Lights*, his American publisher couldn't be convinced to switch from the one it had erroneously attached to the book.

Ironically, the first British edition appeared with a picture of the alethiometer on the front cover, and the first American edition had a picture of the polar bear Iorek Byrnison. It might have made more sense the other way around. And as strong as those illustrations are, Pullman had another in mind when he first thought of alluding to Milton's "golden compasses." It is, as Pullman says, "one of the most immediately recognizable images in the whole of Western art." It's a drawing by the great Milton admirer William Blake. Though Blake didn't give it a title, it's often called "Ancient of Days"—a name for God that Pullman also uses in *His Dark Materials*. Blake drew it to accompany his poem "Europe," one of the works that explains his mythology and his prophecies for the world. (Blake would probably have said the figure is his alternative version of God, known as Urizen. More about Blake and his influence on Pullman in the next chapter.)

As Pullman has said, "Whatever its origin,

"At the time, I didn't have enough clout to resist," Pullman has said about the title change for the American market.

Ancient of Days (1794)
William Blake

this design is so powerful that it's broken free of its context altogether. . . ." He adds that it has "a natural and immediate connection with the passage in Book VII of *Paradise Lost*."

But once again Pullman gave the allusion a twist. In Milton's passage, and in Blake's illustration, God is creating the world. In Pullman's world, God isn't the Creator. Pullman makes the allusion because it comes from the same general set of ideas—an interest in religious thought—and it evokes the mood he wanted for *His Dark Materials*. It also pleases him that it brings Milton and Blake together, because Blake's view of Milton—that Milton is "of the Devil's party without knowing it"—shaped Pullman's.

FALL BACK, SPRING FORWARD

Those emotional echoes of Milton are as important to Pullman as the intellectual ones. He felt them long before he began assembling elements for his story. They were strong enough to sustain his momentum through the seven years he wrote *His Dark Materials*. And it's the source of those emotions, more than individual quotations, that's fundamental to Milton's influence on Pullman. Speaking about the story of Eve's temptation and the

Milton! thou shouldst be living at this hour: England hath need of thee: she is a fen Of stagnant waters; altar, sword, and pen, Fireside, the heroic wealth of hall and bower, Have forfeited their ancient English dower Of inward happiness. We are selfish men . . . Thy soul was like a Star, and dwelt apart . . .
—William Wordsworth, "England, 1802"

23

After *Paradise Lost,* Milton wrote *Paradise Regained* (1671). It's sometimes called the "brief epic." (It's ten thousand words, compared to the eighty thousand of *Paradise Lost.*) It retells the Bible stories of Satan's efforts to tempt Jesus. Because Jesus resists, writes Milton, "Eden [is] raised in the wasted wilderness." (*Paradise Regained,* Book I, line 7)

banishment of Adam and Eve from paradise, Pullman said, "I think it's the central myth of our human nature; it explains us, and our conscience, and our consciousness, with more power and elegance and richness of implication than any other story I know." And in his opinion, "There's never been a greater version of it" than *Paradise Lost.*

Yet despite his great respect for Milton, Pullman truly does reverse the moral polarities. Whether or not Milton ends up with the Devil's party, his story's opening lines clearly set out the idea that Adam and Eve

Brought death into the World, and all our woe.

Pullman couldn't disagree more. He doesn't believe the story of Eve's temptation is a disgraceful episode of human weakness. He doesn't believe it's a descent from virtue and innocence to evil and sin.

What Christianity calls the Fall of Man, says Pullman, "is the best thing, the most important thing that ever happened to us, and if we had our heads straight on this issue, we would have churches dedicated to Eve instead of the Virgin Mary."

As blasphemous as that sounds, there's

actually a tradition in religious scholarship of thinking the Fall of Man was a good thing—a "Fortunate Fall" or "Felix Culpa" (Latin for "fortunate fault"). Milton himself believed that. But Pullman's idea of Felix Culpa is a little different, and it's important to make the distinction.

When people talk about the Fortunate Fall, they imply that Adam and Eve's sin led to humanity's existence, so we're alive and can devote ourselves to God. As Milton put it at the end of *Paradise Lost*:

> O Goodness infinite, Goodness immense!
> . . . evil turn to good; more wonderful
> Than that which by creation first brought
>   forth . . .
> To God more glory, more good-will to Men
>   from God
> (*Paradise Lost*, Book XII, 469–472, 477)

Pullman may be happy that Adam and Eve began the begat, but he doesn't cry with joy at the prospect of giving God more glory. He has said he thinks it's "pessimistic and defeatist" to think "there's no hope of doing any good unless we believe in God and then only if he chooses to bless us with his grace."

What Pullman finds truly fortunate in the

From the Dept. of Wasted Time: Scholars have actually spent time debating whether the Tree of Knowledge from which Eve plucked the Forbidden Fruit was really an apple tree. Apple trees didn't exist in the Middle East. (And that would have stopped God?) Top candidate: a fig tree. The apple may have become a symbol because in Latin the word for apple, *malum*, also means evil.

25

After this book
was completed,
Oxford University
Press published
an illustrated
edition of
*Paradise
Lost* with an
introduction
and explanatory
notes from
Pullman. It's
recommended.
For a closer
look at the
poem, Pullman
recommends
Alastair Fowler's
annotated
edition (1998),
published by
Longman.

story of the Fall of Man—and remember that for Pullman it's a story, not historical fact—is the act of defiance that compels us to seek wisdom because innocence is no longer possible. According to Genesis 3:24, God sent an angel with a flaming sword to block the way back into Eden.

Pullman believes Eve made the right choice. He believes the consequence isn't merely that we can make the best of a bad thing, but that we're free to make the same choice Eve made. That's Milton in reverse.

HOW DID WILLIAM BLAKE INFLUENCE LYRA'S STORY?

At the end of *The Amber Spyglass*, when Pullman includes William Blake among the literary "debts" he acknowledges "above all the rest," he's referring to more than Blake's interpretations of John Milton's *Paradise Lost*. While *Paradise Lost* influenced the structure and themes of Pullman's *His Dark Materials*, Blake's work had an even greater influence on Pullman's personal beliefs. "His work has always been very important to me," says Pullman, "and I consider him one of the greatest writers and indeed artists who ever lived. I read him constantly and continue to be amazed." On his website, Pullman says rereading Blake during the writing of *His Dark Materials* helped him "maintain a vision."

That says a lot about how times change.

William Blake
(1757–1827)

When Blake was alive, many people thought his visions were a sign of insanity.

Blake's reputation is much better today, but his ideas can still shock. In fact, some of the most controversial ideas in *His Dark Materials* are ones Pullman developed while reading Blake. And just as Blake was once attacked for them, now Pullman is.

Go Forth and Sin No More

Like Pullman, Blake rejected Christian ideas of sin—especially original sin, the notion that every human, as the descendant of Adam and Eve, is born with the taint of Eve's failure to resist temptation in the Garden of Eden.

"All Bibles or sacred codes," Blake wrote in *The Marriage of Heaven and Hell*, make the "error" of treating good and evil as opposites. Religions, he believed, incorrectly divide humankind into body and soul, then make the further mistake of declaring the soul sacred and the body profane. Religions are wrong, said Blake, to conclude that "God will torment Man in Eternity" for physical desires.

The divison of body and soul is false, Blake believed, because humankind is *all* soul. He declared, "Man has no Body distinct from his Soul for that called Body is a portion of Soul

From childhood on, Blake believed he saw and spoke with various spirits, including the angel Gabriel and the Virgin Mary.

discerned by the five Senses." In other words, when we use our senses, we're using our souls. So denying the body isn't a way to worship God.

In Blake's philosophy, our desires, which religions tell us to ignore, are the expression of the force that gives us life. Blake called this force "Energy." "Energy is the only life and is from the Body," he wrote. "Energy is Eternal Delight." God doesn't punish us for having Energy.

Blake believed that what religions call good is nothing more than the "passive" side of our souls—the side "that obeys Reason":

> Those who restrain desire, do so because theirs is weak enough to be restrained; and the restrainer or reason usurps its place & governs the unwilling.
>
> (*The Marriage of Heaven and Hell*, plate 5)

Although Reason is Energy's opposite, it doesn't come from a different source, the way Christian virtue comes from God while sin is from Satan. In Blake's philosophy, Reason is nothing more than the outer edge of the soul's Energy, where it becomes weaker. Religious rules that demand obedience are wrong, because they restrain Energy.

Blake illustrated and engraved his poems himself, with an unusual method that combined words and pictures on one acid-etched plate. This "infernal method," as he called it, created a unity he thought important. The process, he said, was explained to him by the spirit of his deceased brother.

"A Grain of Sand in Lambeth That Satan Cannot Find"

In his lifetime, few people would have guessed Blake would be revered by later generations. Most people thought he was a crank. He survived, barely, on the fringes of the art world. Other artists laughed at stories about him, like the time a visitor supposedly found Blake and Blake's wife, Catherine, in their garden reading *Paradise Lost* in the nude. "It's only Adam and Eve," Blake is said to have explained. Naturally, some of the stories were exaggerated. But there was a simple truth in all of them: Blake was an outsider, partly by nature and partly by choice. His unwillingness to cater to the styles of the day prevented him from doing the usual work that supported artists—assisting with commercial engraving, or painting society portraits. Blake preferred to work at his own workshop, which he established in Lambeth, then considered outside central London. He and his wife were able to produce books from start to finish by themselves—a degree of artistic freedom that was more important to Blake than commercial success. In *Jerusalem*, he wrote, "There is a grain of sand in Lambeth that Satan cannot find."

Blake survived thanks to a few patrons and because, for all his eccentricities, he was considered gentle rather than frightening. One friend wrote that, despite being "somewhat taken aback by the boldness of some of [Blake's] assertions," the friend "never saw anything the least like madness, for I never opposed him spitefully, as many did—but being really anxious to fathom, if possible, the amount of truth which might be in his most startling assertions, I generally met with a sufficiently rational explanation in the most really friendly and conciliatory tone."

For a time, Blake was a follower of Emanuel Swedenborg (1688–1772), who had been a scientist and engineer before becoming a mystic philosopher. Like Blake, Swedenborg believed he spoke with angels and other spirits. When other followers began to establish a Swedenborgian church with layers of authority, Blake rejected the philosophy.

In *His Dark Materials*, Pullman alludes to these ideas a few times. In *The Subtle Knife*, when the witch Lena Feldt and her daemon are attacked by a Specter under orders from Mrs. Coulter, Feldt "feels a hideous and sickening despair" that makes her doubt her beliefs, which read as if they come straight from Blake: "Her last conscious thought was disgust at life; her senses had lied to her. The world was not made of energy and delight but of foulness, betrayal and lassitude." (*The Subtle Knife*, 313) In *The Amber Spyglass*, when Will confronts Mrs. Coulter in the cave where she's holding Lyra, Will sees her face "full of joy and life and energy" as she imagines her plans. (*The Amber Spyglass*, 156)

Pullman's views don't follow every detail of Blake's, but his attitude toward the idea of sin is as negative. In *The Amber Spyglass*, Pullman ridicules that idea when he describes Father Gomez's reaction to the mulefa: "The first thing to do here would be to convince the four-legged creatures, who seemed to have the rudiments of reason, that their habit of riding on wheels was abominable and Satanic, and contrary to the will of God. Break them of that, and salvation would follow." (*The Amber Spyglass*, 464)

Soul Man

The literary critic Alfred Kazin made an observation about Blake that applies to Pullman. "He did not believe in God; under all his artistic labors and intellectual heresies he seems to have thought of nothing else." Pullman describes himself this way:

I have to consider myself an atheist. But because of my upbringing I'm a Christian atheist, and I'm a Church [of England] atheist. And I'm very specifically—because I was brought up in my grandfather's household and he was a Church of England priest when the old prayer book was used—a 1662 Book of Common Prayer atheist, a Hymns Ancient and Modern atheist, and King James Bible atheist.

I know the Bible and the hymn book and the prayer book very, very well, and they form a deep and inescapable part of my nature. I don't want to be free of them. I value enormously my past and my background, and the education I had in a very Christian household.

But I find it impossible to believe.

"All deities reside in the human breast."
—*The Marriage of Heaven and Hell,* plate 11

Blake's works offer a lot to a "Christian atheist" like Pullman. Blake embraced essential Judeo-Christian ethics like "Love thy neighbor as thyself" (Leviticus 19:18), and his focus on spirituality was constant. But he attacked the church for teachings that he considered false and self-serving. He believed the church used doctrines like original sin to oppress believers. He believed religious and political leaders of his time conspired to protect their own comfort while leaving citizens and churchgoers in squalor. His poem "London," for example, condemns both church and state:

> *How the Chimney-sweepers cry*
> *Every blackning Church appalls,*
> *And the hapless Soldiers sigh*
> *Runs in blood down Palace walls . . .*

Pullman's descriptions of the Magisterium in *His Dark Materials* parallel Blake's beliefs.

Some of the Blake works that Pullman reread while working on *His Dark Materials* have themes similar to Pullman's. Like Pullman, Blake created a complex mythology that turned the Christian gospels upside down, telling the story as a struggle for liberation from a false authority. And Blake's works, like Pullman's,

"Unlike many other conscious beings," says Pullman, the mulefa in *His Dark Materials* "never developed a link between knowledge and sin. That was perhaps because they know how to manage their world without exploiting it to the point of ruin." In other words, the mulefa never stopped thinking of nature as natural.

were influenced by scenes in *Paradise Lost*. In Blake's mythology, a character named Orc, who is something like a good version of Milton's Satan, is imprisoned by a false God. Orc breaks free and then frees humanity from the false God's demand for obedience.

Like Pullman, Blake rejected all-or-nothing answers about righteousness and sin. Where traditional Christians like C. S. Lewis might see a choice that leaves a person either on God's side or on Satan's, Blake saw naturally opposing forces that must be balanced. Blake called them "contraries." His notions of "Reason" and "Energy" are examples. He writes, "Without Contraries [there] is no progression. Attraction and Repulsion, Reason and Energy, Love and Hate, are necessary to Human existence."

The mistake, Blake believed, was to judge one of the pair good and the other evil. That only separates them, preventing humankind from progressing as individuals or as a society. Our goal should be to bring these contraries together, as in his philosophy of body and soul. The separation of body and soul is unnatural, because they are really the same thing. They must be united for a person to live at peace.

How can that be achieved? As Alfred Kazin

Fans of J. R. R. Tolkien's *The Lord of the Rings* may be wondering if there's a connection between Blake's character Orc and the Orcs who are the ghoulish troops on the side of evil in Tolkien's trilogy. No, there's not. Tolkien took the name from an Anglo-Saxon word for monster. He wasn't thinking of Blake at all, and Blake's Orc isn't ghoulish.

explains, Blake believed that, "With the aid of vision, and through the practice of art, man bursts through the contraries and weds them together by his own creativity."

Pullman thinks and works much the same way. When I asked him about his habit of bending his allusions, sometimes giving them a meaning opposite of the original, he said, "I have a horror of trying to write something in order to fit some existing scheme." Then he quoted a line from Blake's poem *Jerusalem*:

I must create my own system or be enslaved by another man's.

The next line of *Jerusalem* is just as apt:

I will not Reason & Compare: my business is to Create

In religious terms that even Father Gomez would understand, Blake and Pullman share a central belief: Create, and salvation will follow.

AND THEY CALL IT PUPPY LOVE

References to Blake are scattered throughout *His Dark Materials*. Some are just faint echoes of memorable phrases from Blake's poems. At the beginning of the confrontation between Will and Mrs. Coulter in the cave in *The Amber Spyglass*, Pullman describes Will's perception of Mrs. Coulter's duplicity: "She sounded so kindly, and there was such sad wisdom in her eyes, that Will's mistrust deepened. He felt that every word she said was a lie, every action concealed a threat, and every smile was a mask of deceit." (*The Amber Spyglass*, 139) That's an allusion to the first lines of a Blake poem, "The Smile" (1807):

> *There is a smile of love*
> *And there is a smile of deceit . . .*

A more important allusion is repeated throughout *His Dark Materials*. It's connected to an element of Blake's philosophy that Pullman had in mind when shaping Lyra's character and writing the love story between Lyra and Will.

Several times, Pullman mentions Lyra's growth from "innocence" to "experience." Those words come straight from the titles of Blake's most famous series of poems, *Songs of Innocence* and *Songs of Experience*.

Most of the poems in those two collections are arranged as mirror images of the same incident or emotion, with contrasting

Blake wasn't as absolute as C.S. Lewis describes in *The Great Divorce* (see sidebar, opposite). Lewis made him seem unreasonable to win the argument. But there was a real difference between them: Lewis believed there is only one route to God, through Jesus (and preferably the Anglican church, because Lewis thought some other Christians strange). Blake believed other ways were possible.

LYRA BELACQUA: LITTLE GIRL LOST

If you don't know her by now, you will never, ever know her. Digging for subtle allusions in Lyra's story won't reveal deep secrets.

Asking Pullman won't change anything. Having written more than a thousand pages about Lyra, it's natural that he says *his* creation is what counts, not an earlier idea or character.

He has said something like the following in many interviews:

Lyra's a very ordinary little girl. There are hundreds of Lyras in Oxford. I used to teach Lyras when I was teaching. There were thousands and millions of children like Lyra, and Will, in every country in the world. There's nothing special about her. She's only special by virtue of the fact that at some point she will be placed in a particular situation where the fate of a lot of things depends on what she does. It's not her, it's not special to her: she's a very ordinary child. And this is something which I stress throughout, and especially in the third book.

Pullman may be overstating it. It's true that Lyra hasn't inherited special magical powers, which distinguishes her from many other fantasy fiction characters. But she's still a Child of Destiny, the subject of a prophecy—and not a small one. In fact, from the moment Pullman introduces us to Lyra, he shows us she's special. She's related to important members of society. She's a leader among her peers. She's braver than most of them.

As soon as we meet her, we know she might be more than "a very ordinary little girl," because Pullman has given her a very unordinary name. He's often asked about that. Where did "Lyra" come from? What does it mean? Pullman says, "It just popped into my head, really. I don't think it means anything [to the story], and if it does, I don't know what it might mean." Although he knew the word—the term for a small harp and the name of a constellation, he adds,

I'd never heard it used as a name. As far as my writing of the story is concerned, it just appeared with the girl. As soon as she was there, I knew she was Lyra.

Nonetheless, once the name existed, Pullman did notice a connection that he wove into *His Dark Materials*. When Lyra loses her ability to read the alethiometer, Pullman describes her as "a little girl, lost." (*The Subtle Knife*, 160) That's a phrase from some William

Blake poems. One, titled "The Little Girl Lost," is about a girl called Lyca. (Scholars have often wondered about Blake's choice of that name. Since it seems to come from the Latin word for wolf, some scholars say Blake chose it to show his character is a wild child.) In that poem, Lyca falls asleep in the wild, and

> *. . . beasts of prey,*
> *Come from caverns deep,*
> *Viewed the maid asleep*

Later, the animals

> *. . . conveyed*
> *To caves the sleeping maid.*

Pullman's Lyra, you remember, is sleeping in a cave in the beginning of *The Amber Spyglass*.

Even stronger connections between Lyra and Blake's work are apparent in a second Blake poem with almost the same title: Instead of "*The* Little Girl Lost," it's "*A* Little Girl Lost." It tells about the unnatural linking of love and sin. The girl and a boy meet "in a garden bright," just as Lyra and Will meet at midday in Oxford's Botanic Garden. Wanting more than a chaste romance, Blake's characters plan to meet "when the silent sleep/ waves o'er heaven's deep"—a line playfully echoed in Pullman's description of the

"silent sleeping city by the sea"
that Mary Malone finds. (*The
Subtle Knife*, 254) The girl has a
white-haired father who doesn't
want her to grow up and experience what he considers sin.
Blake ends the poem with an
entreaty to the young girl to
stand up for her natural desires.

A LITTLE GIRL LOST

Children of the future age,
Reading this indignant page,
Know that in a former time
Love, sweet love, was
    thought a crime.

In the age of gold,
Free from winter's cold,
Youth and maiden bright,
To the holy light,
Naked in the sunny
    beams delight.

Once a youthful pair,
Filled with softest care,
Met in garden bright
Where the holy light
Had just removed the
    curtains of the night.

There, in rising day,
On the grass they play;
Parents were afar,
Strangers came not near,
And the maiden soon
    forgot her fear.

Tired with kisses sweet,

They agree to meet
When the silent sleep
Waves o'er heaven's deep,
And the weary tired
    wanderers weep.

To her father white
Came the maiden bright;
But his loving look,
Like the holy book,
All her tender limbs
    with terror shook.

Ona, pale and weak,
To thy father speak!
O the trembling fear!
O the dismal care
That shakes the
    blossoms of my hoary hair!

"The Girl for Me"

Were all the inspirations for Lyra intellectual? Not quite. On his website, Pullman says Lyra has been around in one form or another since his childhood:

Among the "proper" books I loved, there are some that I still read. . . . I remember a novel called *A Hundred Million Francs,* by the French author Paul Berna. It was a good story, about a bunch of children in a dingy suburb of Paris who find a lot of money which has been hidden by some thieves, and all kinds of adventures follow. The point about that book for me was that on page 34, there was a drawing of some of the kids defying the crooks, and I fell in love with the girl in the drawing. She was a tough-looking, very French sort of character, with a leather jacket and socks rolled down to her ankles and blonde hair and black eyes, and altogether I thought she was the girl for me. I wouldn't be at all surprised—in fact, now I think about it, it's obvious—to find that the girl on page 34 of *A Hundred Million Francs* is the girl who four decades later turned up in my own book *Northern Lights,* or *The Golden Compass,* where she was called Lyra.

The British edition of *A Hundred Million Francs* was illustrated by Richard Kennedy.

Some Blake lines
from a work
titled *Milton:
a Poem* (1804)
were set to
music in 1916
and are now
an unofficial
national anthem
in Britain. They
talk about the
legend, which
Blake believed,
that Jesus
visited Britain.
They begin:
"And did those
  feet in ancient
  time
Walk upon
  England's
  mountains
  green?
And was the holy
  Lamb of God
On England's
  pleasant
  pastures
  seen?"

perceptions that reveal the difference between innocent and experienced views of the world. For example, in "The Little Boy Found," a poem from *Songs of Innocence*, a lost child is guided back to his mother by God. But the same child, in the mirror poem in *Songs of Experience*, instead encounters one of God's earthly representatives—a cruel priest. It's titled "A Little Boy Lost."

Blake saw this growth from innocence to experience as natural and inevitable. Nice as it would be to have a completely innocent view of the world, it wouldn't be accurate. And we'd only be able to maintain it by ignoring the evidence of our experience.

That's Pullman's belief too, and an important way of looking at *His Dark Materials*. Pullman has said many times that "the story as a whole is about growing up, or innocence and experience." Lyra begins the story in a state of innocence about the adult world, and spends much of the first scene inside a womb-like closet. Thrown into the adult world, her character grows as she rushes from one intense experience to another: she's introduced to treachery by Mrs. Coulter; she discovers good and evil aren't simple storybook principles when her effort to do good leads to a friend's death; she's taught lessons in friendship and heroism by the bear Iorek Byrnison; and finally, she begins an adult relationship with Will.

This idea, central to *His Dark Materials*, is connected to the interpretation of *Paradise Lost* mentioned earlier. In Pullman's view, the the fall of Adam and Eve from a state of innocence was a good thing, because it was the first step toward achieving real wisdom.

The same man said to have taken Jesus to Britain, Joseph of Arimathea, is sometimes said to have buried the Holy Grail in Glastonbury on a return trip.

SEE NO EVIL: SPECTERS IN PULLMAN AND BLAKE

Readers of *His Dark Materials* who dip into Blake may encounter what seem to be familiar creatures: Specters. Blake's version and Pullman's version aren't the same, but there are interesting similarities.

THE UNKINDEST CUT
Everything you need to know about Pullman's Specters—all of which you were probably afraid to ask—is spelled out in *His Dark Materials*. The short version: the invisible creatures began to be released from the Abyss when the Cittàgazze guild made the Subtle Knife. They sneak through holes the knife cuts between worlds. They suck your soul the way "vampires feast on blood" and leave you senseless. (*The Subtle Knife*, 280)

In storytelling terms, Pullman's Specters are meant to show the danger of Dust draining into the Abyss. Instead of just asking readers to remember Dust is draining away, Pullman has created characters that bring the trouble to Lyra and Will. What a Specter does to one victim, the loss of Dust may do to several worlds.

DOUBLE NEGATIVES
Blake's Spectres (Blake spelled it British style) were more than

As in this page from *Jerusalem,* Blake often drew Spectres as winged creatures. (*Jerusalem,* plate 37)

interesting characters. They were real, and something of an obsession. Blake scholar W. H. Stevenson explains, "'Spectre' is a core word, indicating much that was evil . . . formless, dark, threatening. It is an empty human form, near to a 'Non-Entity.'"

Blake's Spectres, rather than coming from another world, come from within an individual. They're one of four parts of the human psyche, released into the world to exist independently. They're loosed because humankind artificially divides the complex human soul into simple categories of good and evil. From what should be a balanced psyche, four separate forms appear. The Humanity is the part that represents the essential character. It sleeps when the character is divided. The Emanation is the feminine side of character, divided from the male (as in the creation of Eve from Adam). The Shadow is the aspect that represents repressed desire. The Spectre is devoted exclusively to reason. Blake scholar Joseph Hogan explains,

The Spectre functions to define and separate the individual from others. The Spectre acts as guardian and protector of the Emanation. When it is

separated, it is reason, trying to define everything in terms of unchanging essences. It tries to freeze Eternity in a single state. It becomes the Selfhood, trying to impose an immutable and thus false identity on the individual. It resists change, growth, and the very creativity which is the true nature of the Humanity.

Blake's Spectres, like Pullman's Specters, have an insatiable appetite. As Blake writes in *The Four Zoas* (1797):

> *Thou knowest that the Spectre is*
> *in Every Man insane brutisht*
> *Deformd that I am thus*
> *a ravening devouring*
> *lust continually*
> *Craving & devouring ...*

It's possible that lines like these from Blake influenced Pullman; but it's important to understand that Pullman's creations are very different. The greatest difference is that a Spectre in Blake's world becomes, as Blake puts it, "A murderer of its own Body." Pullman's Specters consume the consciousness of other creatures.

FROM BLAKE'S "MY SPECTRE AROUND ME NIGHT AND DAY"

My Spectre around me
    night and day
Like a wild beast guards my way;
My Emanation far within
Weeps incessantly for my sin.

A fathomless and boundless deep,
There we wander, there we weep;
On the hungry craving wind
My Spectre follows thee behind.

He scents thy footsteps
    in the snow
Wheresoever thou dost go,
Thro' the wintry hail and rain.
When wilt thou return again?

Dost thou not in pride and scorn
Fill with tempests all my morn,
And with jealousies and fears
Fill my pleasant nights
    with tears?

Seven of my sweet loves thy knife
Has bereavèd of their life.
Their marble tombs I
    built with tears,
And with cold and
    shuddering fears.

Seven more loves weep
    night and day

Round the tombs where
    my loves lay,
And seven more loves
    attend each night
Around my couch with
    torches bright.

And seven more loves in my bed
Crown with wine my
    mournful head,
Pitying and forgiving all
Thy transgressions great
    and small.

When wilt thou return and view
My loves, and them to life renew?
When wilt thou return and live?
When wilt thou pity
    as I forgive?...

47

WHAT MAKES IOREK BYRNISON SO SMART?

"You cannot trick a bear," Iorek Byrnison tells Lyra. (*The Golden Compass*, 225) He then proves it by asking her to fence with him. Every time she makes a real thrust, he parries it. Every time she tries to trick him with a feint, he knows what she's doing and doesn't move. His skill, he explains, comes from "not being human." Bears, he says, "can see tricks and deceit as plain as arms and legs. We can see in a way humans have forgotten." (*The Golden Compass*, 226)

The fencing episode is one way Pullman acknowledges an important contribution to the ideas in *His Dark Materials*. A short philosophy essay uses a scene with a fencing bear to illustrate an idea that was a major influence on Pullman.

Iorek's name is pronounced YOR-ick, like the former court jester mentioned in Shakespeare's *Hamlet*. Hamlet remembers that his late friend Yorick "hath borne me on his back a thousand times," something Iorek does with Lyra.

The essay was written by German author Heinrich von Kleist (1777–1811). "Kleist," exclaims Pullman, "says in three or four pages what I had to say in 1,300 or so, and says it better. I can't tell you what an impression that essay made on me, and how profound and important I think it is." Setting aside Pullman's comment that Kleist's essay is superior to *His Dark Materials*, it's worth looking into the ideas that affected Pullman so deeply.

Cogito Ergo Sum

The essay is titled "On the Marionette Theater." It's written casually, as if Kleist is telling a story. First he talks about meeting a friend who tells him about the performance of marionettes in a puppet theater. The friend tells him that what made the performance so beautiful was the fact that the marionettes moved as if no conscious effort was involved. Then Kleist talks about a boy who, by chance, bends down in the same pose as a figure in a beautiful statue, but loses his ability to hold the pose the moment he's aware of it. Finally Kleist gives the example of the fencing bear, which he words as if it's a story told to him by a friend:

Kleist also wrote drama and fiction.

> Thrusts and feints followed thick and fast, the sweat poured off me, but in vain. It

wasn't merely that he parried my thrusts like the finest fencer in the world; when I feinted to deceive him he made no move at all. No human fencer could equal his perception in this respect. He stood upright, his paw raised ready for battle, his eye fixed on mine as if he could read my soul there, and when my thrusts were not meant seriously he did not move.

All three stories are meant to explain the consequences of humankind's ability to think at a higher level than other animals. When we do, says Kleist, we lose our grace—our ability to be effortlessly and unconsciously perfect, the way a bear fences perfectly without thinking about it. Kleist says, "Grace appears most purely in that human form which either has no consciousness or an infinite consciousness. That is, in the puppet or in the god." The bear, lacking human self-consciousness, is closer to the puppet. Humans, like the boy who accidentally fell into a statue's pose, have grace before they're conscious of what they're doing and thinking.

Why can't we hold on to our grace as we grow up? Idris Parry, professor of modern German literature at the University of Manchester, whose translation of the essay Pullman chanced upon in a newspaper, explained that Kleist believed

Despite Kleist's success, he was unhappy, and he ended his life soon after he wrote "On the Marionette Theater." The circumstance of his death was scandalous. It was a murder-suicide pact — he first shot his lover, who had cancer, before shooting himself. (There were parallels to that scene in some of his works.) Few friends were sympathetic.

our ability to think actually separates us from certain kinds of knowledge:

> [I]f I am aware of myself I must know that I am a separate entity, aware of and therefore apart from my surroundings; but true knowledge must be complete, connected, indivisible; so separation into subject and object, self and surroundings means distance from knowledge, consequently uncertainty and doubt.

Will's last name, Parry, is one way Pullman acknowledges Idris Parry's role in bringing Kleist's work to Pullman's attention.

For Pullman, that idea is directly connected to William Blake's ideas of innocence and experience. Innocence and grace exist before we realize how separate we are from everyone and everything around us. As Pullman put it to children's literature lecturers Wendy Parsons and Catriona Nicholson, he used to see this happen to his students when he was a teacher:

> They would come to us at the age of nine, sweet and innocent, and by the age of thirteen, they were knowing—knuckles were brushing the ground, all self-conscious, spots, breasts . . . everything was wrong, they were all embarrassed. We lose this state of being, but as Kleist goes on to say, and this is the thing that really excited

me, this is not something to lament, because there's a sort of spectrum here. At one end, there is the inanimate grace of the puppet; at the other end, however, is the fully conscious, fully animate grace of the god. Between, there is human life. We lose the innocence that we were born with, and we then go on through life.

But if we work hard, and if we train ourselves like a dancer, if we undergo all kinds of discipline, pain, suffering, and so forth, then the point is that we can regain grace. We can gain a sort of grace. And the grace of the human dancer who has lost the initial grace but regained it through training is actually a more valuable thing to have, because when you look at the dancer, not only do you see the grace and beauty, you also look into her eyes, and you see wisdom as well. So you can get, if not all the way, at least part of the way, to the state of being a god. And this is what I find so gripping and so optimistic about this particular vision.

Literary critic Alfred Kazin describes Blake's idea with terms similar to the ones Parry uses to explain Kleist: "Innocence is belief, experience is doubt."

In Kleist's words, "we must eat again of the tree of knowledge in order to return to the state of innocence." Kleist's idea goes right back to Pullman's nontraditional views about the Fall

of Man, and to *His Dark Materials* being a
version of *Paradise Lost* with the "moral polarities" reversed. As Pullman says, Kleist's view,
and his, is

> in contrast to C. S. Lewis's idea, for exam-
> ple, the Christian idea, that the Fall is a
> terrible thing; that we are all children of
> sin, and there's no hope of doing any good
> unless we believe in God and then only
> if he chooses to bless us with his grace.
> I think that's a pessimistic and defeatist
> view, and I don't like it at all. I much pre-
> fer Kleist's view. This is the theme of the
> book, of my trilogy.

In Greek
and Roman
mythology, the
Graces are three
sisters who
grant charm
and beauty to
humans.

Lyra's ability with the alethiometer expresses
the same ideas. Being an innocent child, Lyra
can read the alethiometer thanks to "grace." As
Pullman explained in one interview, "Grace is
a mysterious quality which is inexplicable in
its appearance and disappearance. Its disappearance in Lyra's case symbolizes the loss of
innocence but the fact that she can regain it
through work and study symbolizes the fact
that only when we lose our innocence can we
take our first steps towards gaining wisdom."

Pullman isn't merely saying that we can
replace our perfect innocence with wisdom

that's almost as good. He's saying wisdom is better. It's how we reach a new state of grace that, being our own achievement, is even more valuable than the one we enjoyed as children.

"Working toward that end should be a joyful action," says Pullman.

IS LORD ASRIEL THE STORY'S HERO?

Shocked by that idea? Asriel, anyone can see, is the villian. If *His Dark Materials* can be read as a new version of the story of Adam and Eve, surely Asriel is Satan.

Except it's not nearly that simple.

Pullman would say that Asriel isn't Satan, or even evil. In fact there's another model for Asriel, a type of hero that has appeared in myth and literature for thousands of years.

HE LOVES ME, HE LOVES ME NOT

Before the final volume of *His Dark Materials* was published, a puzzled reader asked Pullman what might seem like a simple question: "Whose side is Lord Asriel on—Lyra's or Mrs. Coulter's?" That reader's confusion is understandable. What we see of Asriel comes mostly

Satan was not always depicted as the embodiment of evil. In the Old Testament he is often more of a prosecuting attorney for God, testing humankind's goodness. Later writers decided he was also the serpent in Eden who tempted Eve.

through Lyra's eyes, and she's confused by him right from the start. He's a relative whom she admires, and she believes she can trust him. But quickly she begins to question her judgment. Even after she prevents his murder, he threatens her and keeps secret his plans in the North. Later, when he kills her friend Roger, she thinks she knows: Asriel is evil. Yet after this she wavers.

Pullman skirted the puzzled reader's question. "I know whose side he's on," Pullman said, "and it's not necessarily Lyra's. He's not against her, but he's not for her necessarily." He wasn't just trying to keep his ending secret. It's the truth.

Asriel is on Asriel's side. Asriel doesn't think in terms of being for or against Lyra. His plans were underway long before Lyra learns of them. There are times when he and Lyra are both fighting the Authority, but that's because of decisions Lyra has made. Pullman says, "What I was trying to do was very much get away from the 'He's called the Dark Lord so he must be evil' idea."

BETTER THE DEVIL YOU KNOW
Pullman notes that the question about Asriel is a common one. Readers also weren't sure about the morality of other characters. Before

The northern land in *His Dark Materials*, Svalbard, is a real place. Part of Norway, it's made up of several islands in the Arctic Ocean. Pullman wanted to visit it for research, but at the time he had to apply for an arts grant to cover the travel and he was refused. He relied on photographs instead.

the third book was published, he says, readers used to ask him, "Who's good? Who's bad? Who are we supposed to cheer for?" His response goes to the core of his unorthodox beliefs about good and evil.

I'd always say "Wait till you've got the whole story in front of you, and look at the totality of the character's actions, the part they play in the shape of the whole story, and then you decide." As always, I wasn't going to interpret the story for anyone. In any case, I think that "evil" is something that's easily misunderstood.

Firstly I don't think it exists outside actions in the world: I don't think there's a supernatural principle of evil.

Secondly, I don't think people can be described as evil: they are always too complicated. There are evil actions, certainly, and evil intentions, but while someone is still alive, to call them unequivocally evil is to simplify them (and life) too much. Once they're dead and we can see the whole of what they've done, then maybe.

Stalin, Hitler, Mao [were unequivocally evil] . . .

And thirdly, and importantly, good intentions can lead to evil consequences,

The Dark Lord archetype in literature reflects the common belief that evil in the real world is usually embodied in a single person and requires a high position to be effective. But as political scientist Hannah Arendt pointed out, the Holocaust was as much the result of banal evil perpetuated by bureaucrats who were no different from bureaucrats anywhere.

Some religions, like Christian Science, deny the existence of supernatural evil. This is one solution to the logical problem faced by most religions: if God is all-powerful and all-good, how can evil exist? Is God unable to prevent evil (in which case God isn't all-powerful)? Or does God wish to test us with suffering (in which case God isn't all-good)?

and vice versa. That's why we need to see things in the round, in the context of all their causes and consequences, before we can pronounce a final verdict on whether they're evil or not.

Understanding those ideas is crucial to understanding Pullman as a thinker and as a writer.

Pullman's belief that there's no "supernatural principle of evil" separates him from many religions. Evil, according to most religious traditions, comes from the divine realm. It might be an omnipresent force in the universe that finds its way into people or things, or it might be personified in gods or demons. In nearly every case, it travels from the divine world into ours. That notion goes back to the first recorded religions. The word "devil" is much older than the story of Satan. It comes from the name of evil gods in Zoroastrianism, the religion of ancient Persia.

One unfair criticism of Pullman's beliefs is the complaint that with no divine standards for evil, his characters are morally free to do whatever they please. Any Pullman reader knows that's not the case. While it's true that Pullman's work is essentially humanist—it puts humankind, not God, at the moral center—Pullman's ethics are Judeo-Christian.

Pullman believes you should do unto others as you would have others do unto you. The difference is that his characters are entirely responsible for their failure or success in living up to those standards. In Pullman's world, you don't get to say, "The devil made me do it."

Pullman's rejection of a simple "Dark Lord" role for Asriel is part of his emphasis on learning to see adult complications. He says, "What I would like sensible readers to come away with is something that reminds them of real life, where no-one is purely good or purely evil, and where thinking of people like that is unhelpful anyway. . . . [I]t's just more interesting when someone we think is trustworthy turns out to have feet of clay, or when someone who has been cruel turns out to be moved by love and self-sacrifice."

Asriel's murder of Lyra's friend Roger isn't forgiven by Pullman's code. Pullman considers it an evil act. But it doesn't mean Asriel has a wholly evil character. He's still capable of doing good. And though we can fault his methods, his intention is to free humankind from the Magisterium and the Authority. That desire isn't selfless—by overthrowing the Authority he hopes to gain personal power—but he's aware of the broader good when he commits his evil act. That's the sort of complex ethical

"Azazel" is the name of a demon in the Bible and Satan's standard-bearer in *Paradise Lost*. In Islam, Azazel is the one who defied God and later became known as Shaitan (Satan).

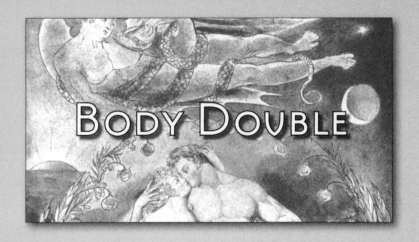

BODY DOUBLE

Lord Asriel forms an army to fight God, but when the battle cry is sounded he actually fights Metatron, a substitute. Why the switch?

You could say it's necessary for the storytelling. The story's message leads logically to the weak God whom Lyra finally meets. However, Metatron is more than a stand-in character. He's an ancient figure from religious tradition, where he plays a role similar to the one he fills in *His Dark Materials*.

MAN OF MYSTERY
Metatron appears in many religious texts, especially those connected to Jewish mysticism. He's sometimes described as the largest of the archangels—"equal to the breadth of the whole world" says one source. Often he's God's right-hand man. Gustav Davidson, collector of angel lore, says in one legend Metatron is a "spirit of fire" with thirty-six pairs of wings and "innumerable eyes." Another source, according Davidson, says when Metatron is invoked he "appears as a pillar of fire, his face more dazzling than the sun."

Because the archangel Michael, in most Christian teaching, has the same characteristics, Metatron is sometimes said to be just Michael with a different name. Other scholars say Metatron was a man named Enoch, raised to great status after death. That's the version Pullman follows when Baruch and Balthamos discuss Metatron with Asriel and Will.

Some scholars credit Metatron with interesting roles played by anonymous angels in the Bible. They say he was the unnamed "man" who wrestled all night with Jacob (Genesis 32). Even more important, they say God sent Metatron to guide the Israelites from Egypt. The text of Exodus 23:22 reads: "See, I am sending an angel ahead of you to guard you along the way and to bring you to the place I have prepared. Pay attention to him and listen to what he says. Do not rebel against him; he will not forgive your rebellion, since my Name is in him."

There are scholars who consider the reference to God's name to be a clue to a code. Numerologists, who assign numbers to each letter of the alphabet, say the digits assigned to Metatron's Hebrew name add up to the same total as the digits in the Hebrew name of God. They say this means Metatron is the guardian angel mentioned in Exodus.

Making a List, Checking It Twice

In religious tradition, Metatron is more than a substitute player. He has two crucial roles of his own.

The first is the angel of death. Metatron keeps track of when everyone is supposed to die, dispatching other angels to take a dead person's soul at just the right moment.

The other is closer to the role he plays in *His Dark Materials*. According to certain branches of Judaism, Metatron is God's Lord Regent on Earth—a "little Adonai" ("little God"). This notion comes from the mystical belief in some sects that there are really two worlds in Creation: an invisible spiritual world and the visible physical world in which we live. God doesn't bother to deal with the physical world, according to this tradition. It's beneath him. He lets Metatron deal with it.

situation that interests Pullman.

Pullman also wanted Lyra to experience a shocking ethical lesson. In trying to save Roger, she puts him in harm's way. She feels partially responsible for his death, and in Pullman's view she should. Pullman believes you can put a twist on the old saying that sometimes bad things happen to good people: Sometimes bad things happen *because of* good people.

John Keats
(1795–1821)

MAD, BAD, AND DANGEROUS TO KNOW

Although Pullman rejected the usual fantasy-literature model of the Dark Lord for Asriel, he did have a literary model in mind.

"I suppose what lay behind my idea of Lord Asriel," Pullman says, "was the generic Romantic hero, and I mean [from the] Romantic [era] rather than romantic."

Pullman is referring to Romanticism, an artistic movement that appeared in the late 1700s and early 1800s, long after Milton's death. Romanticism emphasized emotions and instinct over knowledge and learning. William Blake was a Romantic. John Keats, the poet whom Mary Malone quotes, was a Romantic. His most famous lines, from his poem "Ode on a Grecian Urn," sum up Romanticism neatly: "'Beauty is truth, truth beauty'—that is all ye know on Earth, and all ye need to know." (For more on Keats in *His Dark Materials*, see page 116.) In politics as well as art, Romantics admired rebellion and freedom. They supported the revolutions in America and France.

The classic Romantic hero scorns convention and follows his own moral standards. He's a loner, and pursues his grand ambitions and desires regardless of society's reaction. (I say "he" because the classic examples are all male characters. Mr. Rochester from Charlotte Brontë's *Jane Eyre* may be the best known.)

Lord Byron is credited with shaping the Romantic hero. Some scholars refer to this sort of character as a Byronic hero. (That's partly because Byron scorned convention in his real life too. One of his lovers, Lady Caroline Lamb, the wife of a future prime minister of Britain, famously called him "mad, bad, and dangerous to know." To be fair, the same could have been said of her.) But it's worth noting that Byron was influenced by some female writers who aren't studied widely, in particular Ann Radcliffe (1764–1823), author of several gothic novels. Her books, in which heroines encounter the mysterious and apparently dangerous lords of isolated castles, were considered spooky entertainments. In *The*

George Gordon,
Lord Byron
(1788–1824)

Italian (1797), she describes a Romantic hero as clearly as Byron ever did:

Radcliffe might be more studied today if she weren't so elusive to biographers. She left very little correspondence and no literary journals, the stuff that makes academics swoon. With Byron, on the other hand, it's easy work to compare his dramatic literature to his eventful life.

Among his associates no one loved him, many disliked him, and more feared him. His figure was striking . . . there was something terrible in its air; something almost super-human. An habitual gloom and severity prevailed over the deep lines of his countenance; and his eyes were so piercing that they seemed to penetrate, at a single glance, into the hearts of men, and to read their most secret thoughts; few persons could support their scrutiny, or even endure to meet them twice.

Byron, in his poem *Lara* (1814), describes a man much like both Radcliffe's character and Pullman's Asriel:

In him inexplicably mix'd appeared
Much to be loved and hated, sought and
*   feared;*
Opinion varying o'er his hidden lot ...
There was in him a vital scorn of all:
As if the worst had fall'n which could
*   befall,*
He stood a stranger in this breathing world,
An erring spirit from another hurled;

A thing of dark imaginings, that shaped
By choice the perils he by chance escaped ...
So much he soared beyond, or sunk
    beneath,
The men with whom he felt condemned to
    breathe,
And longed by good or ill to separate
Himself from all who shared his mortal
    state;
His mind abhorring this had fixed her
    throne
Far from the world, in regions of her
    own ...
He had (if 'twere not nature's boon) an art
Of fixing memory on another's heart ...
Vain was the struggle in that mental net,
His spirit seemed to dare you to forget!

"I have a great mind to believe in Christianity for the mere pleasure of fancying I may be damned."
—Lord Byron

In *The Golden Compass*, Lyra senses the same qualities in her father:

> [H]er father was lying back in his chair, lazy and powerful, his eyes as fierce as his daemon's. She didn't love him, she couldn't trust him, but she had to admire him, and the extravagant luxury he'd assembled in this desolate wasteland, and the power of his ambition. (*The Golden Compass*, 376)

Gustav Davidson's *Dictionary of Angels*, a source for Pullman, lists an angel named Azrael—"one of the chief angels of destruction" who in some traditions is "the embodiment of evil." Like Lord Asriel, Azrael commands huge armies of spirits.

Pullman borrowed only the name, not the personal history; but there's one very eerie link, even if it's coincidental or unconscious. See the sidebar opposite.

Describing Asriel's connection to Romanticism, Pullman explains, "It's the theme of the rebellion against authority that matters." He also makes the connection to the way the Romantics viewed *Paradise Lost*. Many agreed with William Blake that the epic can be read as a heroic struggle against an unreasonable authority. Pullman refers to Milton's Satan as the "paradigm" for the Romantic hero.

But don't think Asriel plays Satan's role. It isn't so. While there are similarities between Asriel and Milton's Satan, Pullman hasn't put tracing paper over *Paradise Lost*. The stories are different, and the two characters play different roles in them. Asriel does some of what Satan does, but not all. He's not the first character to resist the Authority. He doesn't tempt Lyra with sin. Those are crucial parts of what supposedly makes Satan evil in *Paradise Lost*. In *His Dark Materials*, other characters perform those acts. Mary Malone tempts Lyra. (See "You Little Devil," page 70.) The first character to challenge the Authority is an angel we never meet in *His Dark Materials*. She'll appear in *The Book of Dust*, which Pullman is writing at the same time I'm writing this book. (More about her later.)

Fire and Ice

The questions Pullman has been asked about Asriel show it can be tricky for a writer to associate a character with Satan. Readers come to such a character with fixed ideas.

Romantic poet Percy Shelley, who also needed to get Satan behind him for a verse play he hoped to write, solved the problem in an interesting way. It shines a different light on Asriel.

Shelley realized the Romantic hero is connected not just to Milton's version of Satan, but also to a character with no evil qualities, Greek mythology's Prometheus.

Prometheus was one of the Titans, gods who ruled before Zeus and the other Olympians overthrew them. (Atlas, who held the world on his shoulders, and from whom we take our word for a book of maps, was another Titan.)

Prometheus was said to love humans more than any other god did. He was the god who created humankind, say some legends. He often defended humans from the wrath of other gods, and taught them many skills.

After the Titans were displaced, Prometheus rebelled against Zeus and the Olympians. He's best known in particular for a single act of defiance. He stole fire from his fellow gods and gave it to humankind as a gift, because

Lord Asriel's treatment of the Gobbler's victims, like Lyra's friend Roger— separating body from daemon— is much like a role played by the angel Azrael, who in some legends is the angel of death. Gustav Davidson says Azrael provided the handfuls of dirt needed to complete the creation of Adam, and as a result "was appointed to separate body from soul."

YOU LITTLE DEVIL

When Lena Feldt, while being tortured, reveals to Mrs. Coulter the prophecy that Lyra will be "Mother Eve" and that Lyra "will disobey" (*The Subtle Knife*, 314), it's reasonable to guess Lyra will face temptation before disobeying, just as Eve is tempted from innocence in the Bible.

Less easy to guess: that Mary Malone will play the role Satan did when he offered Eve an apple from the Tree of Knowledge. Despite the fact that Mary Malone is called "the tempter" several times in the trilogy, it's easy to miss that plot twist. We're accustomed to think of the Fall of Man as

disastrous, the result of Satan's evilness and our weakness. Mary Malone doesn't seem at all Satanic. Asriel does, and he's the character who might be expected to tempt Lyra.

By giving the role of tempter to Mary, Pullman reinforces his belief that the Fall of Man was good for humankind. "The temptation," he has said, "is wholly beneficent." He explains:

[Mary] tells her story about how she fell in love, which gives Lyra the clue as to how to express what she's now beginning to feel about Will, and when it happens they both understand what's going on and are tempted and they (so to speak) fall. But it's a fall into grace, towards wisdom, not something that leads to sin, death, misery, hell—and Christianity.

Here we're coming back to the ideas from William Blake about the movement from innocence to experience. For Pullman, this is an essential step in a full life. You can also see in his choice of Mary as tempter a sign of the first creative spark for *His Dark Materials*, the notion of "reversing the moral polarities" of Milton's *Paradise Lost*. As mentioned earlier, in Milton's poem Satan argued that it's impossible to worship Creation if you don't understand it fully, so by choosing knowledge you are actually taking a step toward the divine, not away from it. Mary comes to the same belief as a scientist rather than a fallen angel, but the result is the same. Her pursuit of knowledge puts her in touch with angels.

DIVIDE AND CONQUER
Children's literature scholar Kristin Cashore found an interesting pattern created by Pullman's choice of Mary as tempter. Noting that Christian theology often speaks of God as a trinity—the Father, the Son, and the Holy Ghost—she says "it is interesting that in

Pullman's novel, God is one (there is no mention of Jesus or the Holy Spirit) and Satan is three." Pullman, she says,

creates a sort of "Satan in three persons." First is the fallen Satan, the rebel angel who opposes God's tyrannous takeover in the beginning and is subsequently banished. This character never appears in person in Pullman's text, but she is referred to as a heroine and as a powerful force in Lord Asriel's rebellion. Second is Lord Asriel, the character most directly aligned with and opposed to Pullman's God figure, "the Authority." Asriel represents power, glory, fury, and a breathtaking ambition. His fortress of glaring fires and smoking furnaces, where he broods and plans his war against God, parallels the depictions of Hell in *Paradise Lost*. Third is Satan the temptress, Mary Malone, an everyday woman who walks among common people and gently influences Lyra and Will's sexual awakening.

Cashore is careful not to suggest Pullman intended this pattern. Pullman confirms that it wasn't his conscious intent at all. Yet it's there, and it's consistent with the themes of the story.

he wanted humans to have the knowledge and power and freedom that the Olympians kept for themselves.

Zeus punished Prometheus for this crime by chaining him to a rock and sending an eagle to peck out and eat his liver. Each day, the liver grew back; each day, the eagle returned. If the hero Hercules hadn't accidentally found him and broken his chains, Prometheus would have suffered on the rock forever.

The disobedience of Prometheus, and the sacrifice he made to bring humans knowledge of fire, has been the subject of countless works of art. Echoes of it are found in other myths, like the Norse legend of the god Odin, who hanged himself from the Tree of Life for many days until he gained the knowledge of reading runes, an alphabet he gave to humankind. Many traditions tell stories about virtuous disobedience against the gods.

Shelley retold the story in a verse play, *Prometheus Unbound* (1820). In his introduction, Shelley explained his reason for choosing an alternative to Satan:

> Prometheus is, in my judgement, a more poetical character than Satan because, in addition to courage and majesty and firm and patient opposition to omnipotent

In Islam, the angel Azrael plays the same role played by Metatron in certain mystical strains of Judaism: he is the angel of death, with a book in which he writes the name of a person at birth and then erases it when it is time for death. (See also "Body Double," p. 62.)

force, he is susceptible of being described as exempt from the taints of ambition, envy, revenge, and a desire for personal aggrandisement, which in the Hero of *Paradise Lost* interfere with the interest [of the reader]. . . . Prometheus is, as it were, the type of the highest perfection of moral and intellectual nature, impelled by the purest and the truest motives to the best and noblest ends.

In some versions of the Prometheus myth, Zeus punished humankind by creating Pandora, the first woman, and giving her the box that released evil into the human world. Pandora is an ancient Greek parallel to the Bible story of Eve and sin.

Freed from the ill will that greets any mention of Satan, Shelley could keep his audience focused on the story's theme, which is similar to a central theme of *His Dark Materials*. Describing Shelley's work, poet and critic George Edward Woodberry explains, "Unable to bring mankind back to primitive innocence, [Prometheus] used knowledge as a weapon to defeat evil, by leading mankind beyond the state wherein they are sinless through ignorance, to that in which they are virtuous through wisdom."

When Pullman is pushed to reduce *His Dark Materials* to one idea, that's precisely it. Of course Asriel isn't as pure and noble as Prometheus. He's full of ambition. And in the end it's Lyra who finds wisdom. But Asriel has some of the same virtuous aims as

Prometheus's name means "forward-thinking." There are many stories about his ability to see how events would turn out and plan accordingly. His brother Epimetheus, whose name means "backward-thinking," lacked Prometheus's intelligence.

Prometheus. He wants knowledge and freedom and progress. In *The Golden Compass,* he explains to Lyra:

> Somewhere out there is the origin of all the Dust, all the death, the sin, the misery, the destructiveness in the world. Human beings can't see anything without wanting to destroy it, Lyra. *That's* original sin. And I'm going to destroy it. Death is going to die. (*The Golden Compass,* 377)

We learn in the end that Asriel doesn't quite understand Dust, and he's far too ruthless for Lyra's taste (or Pullman's). But in fighting the Authority to gain wisdom, Asriel is Promethean. So while it may be a stretch to call him the story's hero, he's undoubtedly heroic.

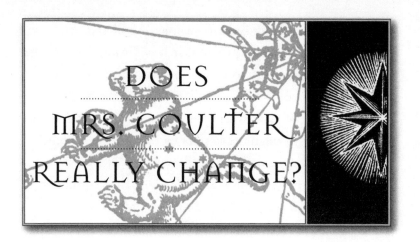

DOES MRS. COULTER REALLY CHANGE?

First she's the character you love to hate. Then she's the character you hate to love. Trying to pin down Mrs. Coulter is like trying to keep hold of the mythological figure Proteus, who instantly turns into one horrible monster after another to escape a captor's grasp.

Pullman says she astonishes him too. "Mrs. Coulter surprised me by turning out the way she did," he says. "She was always one step ahead of me, actually. I could never quite tell how she was going to get out of this circumstance or that one, this situation or that one." He adds, "She's completely free of moral restraint. There's nothing she wouldn't do."

Even her attempts to be good surprised him. Her apparent self-sacrifice in *The Amber*

Independently, both the author of the 2004 stage adaptation, Nicholas Wright, and the costume designer, Jon Morrell, imagined the glamour of actress Marlene Dietrich when they were trying to understand Mrs. Coulter's character.

Spyglass wasn't planned. Pullman explains, "Although I felt that her attitude was changing and deepening or maturing—or whatever you'd like to call it—throughout *His Dark Materials*, it wasn't until I was well on my way through the third book that I realized what she must do in the end."

The revealing detail in that comment is the word "felt." Pullman didn't try to understand everything about Mrs. Coulter when he was writing. "Dealing with her when I was writing the books was always a delicate matter," he explains. "I would approach the matter of her spending time in a cave, for example, with considerable apprehension, and it needed every crumb of diplomatic finesse I could summon to persuade her into a setting so uncomfortable." He still doesn't claim to fully understand her. "In the nine years I have known her, she has never failed to surprise me," he said long after completing *His Dark Materials*.

Pullman also acknowledges that many readers don't trust her even after she appears to change for the better. For many readers, her actions in *The Golden Compass*—abandoning Lyra and heading the child-snatching Gobblers—are too much to forgive. Some think she's just being tricky as usual when she claims in *The Amber Spyglass* to have drugged Lyra for Lyra's own good. Others question the source of her love for Lyra. Dr. Karen S. Coats, a literature professor and Pullman fan, made this interesting point: "I think one of the things that might bother us about Mrs. Coulter is the fact that her mothering, and especially her surge of love at the end, is all tangled up with her narcissism. And while we might not want to admit it, this exposes a basic truth about parenting that we don't like to think about, especially with mothers, who are supposed to be all about others and not about themselves. We are constantly (if unconsciously) scanning our children for bits of ourselves, and this is always implicated in the way we love them."

Readers who distrust Mrs. Coulter's change of heart are both right and wrong. She hasn't really changed, Pullman says. But that's only because the love she shows for Lyra at the end was always there.

Pullman says this is something even he only realized near the end of writing *His Dark Materials*. He says, "She leapt towards what happened in her final scene with such passion that what I'd suspected all the way through was now revealed to be true: that her motives towards Lyra were always protective. Every

In *The Art of Darkness*, Robert Butler's book about the 2004 London stage production, Patricia Hodge, who played Mrs. Coulter, explained the difficulty of the part: "Mrs. Coulter can be perceived as ambiguous, but in playing her I can't be, because nobody is ever ambiguous to themselves. There should be a curious logic to everything she does."

Monkeyshines

Perhaps the only character in *His Dark Materials* more mysterious than Mrs. Coulter is her daemon, the nameless golden monkey. Why did Pullman choose a monkey for her?

The choice combines Pullman's knowledge of literature with pure imagination.

First, imagination. The monkey daemon wasn't planned. The idea came to Pullman as he was writing and simply felt right to him. Only afterward did Pullman think about the possible sources. Even then he didn't dig deep, he says. But he did notice one clear connection, and acknowledges another that's central to his background and to the themes of *His Dark Materials*.

He also realized he'd borrowed the idea from himself. He'd written about an evil monkey once before.

APING HIMSELF?

That earlier monkey appears in Pullman's novel *The Tiger in the Well*. It's a gray monkey with "fierce little eyes" that sits on its master's shoulder, "chattering malevolently." (p. 200)

Pullman says that "sinister monkey . . . itself probably derived from

Ben Wright, actor, with golden monkey puppet created for the 2004
London stage production. Photo copyright © 2004 by Ivan Kyncl.

[Joseph] Sheridan Le Fanu's ghost story 'Green Tea.'"

Le Fanu (1814–1873), from a prominent Anglo-Irish family in Dublin, was popular for his supernatural tales. His vampire novel *Carmilla* influenced Bram Stoker, the author of *Dracula*. More than a dozen versions of it have been filmed. Recent films have also been made from some of his other stories, such as *The Wyvern Mystery*.

In "Green Tea," a man has a frightening nighttime ride on a London omnibus (a large horse-drawn carriage). Two red lights seem to glow inside, and to move as the man moves: "I began now to perceive an outline of something black, and I soon saw, with tolerable distinctness, the outline of a small black monkey, pushing its face forward in mimicry to meet mine; those were its eyes, and I now dimly saw its teeth grinning at me." Things get worse: the "silent, immaterial phantom" keeps returning. Whenever the man says his prayers, the monkey, "with an intense and increasing fury . . . spring[s] on the table, on the back of the chair, on the chimney-piece, and slowly swing[s] itself from side to side, looking at me all the time." (I'm not going to spoil the ending. The story's online.)

Zoo Logic

Another source of monkey imagery for Pullman was William Blake's *Marriage of Heaven and Hell*, which contains this horrible scene:

> I descended driving the Angel before me, soon we saw seven houses of brick, one we enterd; in it were a number of monkeys, baboons, & all of that species chaind by the middle, grinning and snatching at one another, but witheld by the shortness of their chains: however I saw that they sometimes grew numerous, and then The weak were caught by the strong and with a grinning aspect, first coupled with & then devourd, by plucking off first one limb and then another till the body was left a helpless trunk. this after grinning & kissing it with seeming fondness they devourd too; and here & there I saw one savourily picking the flesh off of his own tail . . .

"Yes, I know that passage," Pullman told me when asked about it. "*The Marriage of Heaven and Hell* is one of the central texts of my life. I first read it when I was 15 or so."

"Do you think the impression it left may have contributed to the appearance of Mrs. Coulter's monkey?" I asked.

"Every impression counts!" he replied.

MONKEYING AROUND

Adding to the monkey's threatening mystique, Pullman never even reveals its name. As a result, many Pullman fans were surprised the monkey was called "Ozymandias" in a BBC Radio adaptation. The name is the title of a famous poem by the Romantic poet Percy Bysshe Shelley:

I met a traveller from
an antique land,
Who said: – Two vast and
trunkless legs of stone
Stand in the desert . . . near
them, on the sand,
Half sunk a shattered visage
lies, whose frown,
And wrinkled lips, and sneer
of cold command,
Tell that its sculptor well
those passions read
Which yet survive, stamped
on these lifeless things,
The hand that mocked them,
and the heart that fed;
And on the pedestal these
words appear:
"My name is Ozymandias,
King of Kings,
Look on my Works ye
Mighty, and despair!"
Nothing beside remains.
Round the decay

Of that colossal Wreck,
boundless and bare
The lone and level sands
stretch far away.

Shelley's poem was inspired by a statue of the Egyptian Ramses II (circa 1300 B.C.), which was inscribed, "King of Kings am I, Osymandias. If anyone would know how great I am and where I lie, let him surpass one of my works."

What does the name reveal about Mrs. Coulter's daemon and her personality? Is Pullman suggesting a pitiful attempt to achieve immortality when all things must return to Dust?

No. The name wasn't Pullman's invention at all. It came from the writer who adapted Pullman's story for the BBC. Pullman says, "It was a silly name, and if I'd had the chance I would have vetoed it."

The monkey will remain nameless. As Pullman told one interviewer, "The golden monkey doesn't have a name because every time I tried to think of one, he snarled and frightened me."

I asked him, "Did you even try, or was the feeling clear from the beginning?"

His reply was typical: "I didn't try very hard!"

time she intervenes in Lyra's life, it is to protect her from danger, real or suspected. The very first time she meets Lyra it's in order to take her away from Oxford, where the Gobblers are doing their work: and although it's *her* work, she doesn't want Lyra to suffer from it. So all the time there's a complexity in her motives, which was sometimes too deep for me to fathom. It's why I found her so interesting to write about. . . ."

At the very beginning of *The Amber Spyglass,* observed Dave Weich of the Oregon bookseller Powell's, Mrs. Coulter learns the importance of telling the truth before Lyra does.

What makes Mrs. Coulter so complicated, and so interesting, is that she may not know her true character any better than we or Pullman does. "As far as I know," Pullman says, careful not to presume too much, "I have this to say about Mrs. Coulter, even more than most of my characters: her instincts towards Lyra were indeed always protective; but at the beginning, they were combined with a fierce and resentful irritation, and only gradually and against her conscious will grew into an even fiercer love."

There are several reasons for that irritation. Among them: Lyra's birth altered her relationship with Asriel; Lyra's presence might have stood in the way of her career; she feels guilty for resenting Lyra's birth; Lyra upsets her specific plans; Lyra will be young when she is old, which hurts her vanity; and Lyra, not she, is the child of destiny. If Mrs. Coulter could list all these reasons for us, she'd be less real. We all keep some of our darkest thoughts secret even from ourselves. "If it's lifelike at all," says Pullman, any list of motives "will be mixed and contradictory and half of it will be unknown, just as our reasons and motives are in real life."

Yet Mrs. Coulter's early mixed emotions don't take anything away from her final actions on Lyra's behalf. In fact, Pullman uses interesting references to convey the depth of Mrs. Coulter's feelings.

Dr. Coats points out that Mrs. Coulter speaks of her love for Lyra indirectly, using references to the Bible:

> The references to faith as small as a mustard seed are in Matthew 17:20 and Luke 17:6.

> She [Mrs. Coulter] says her love came to her "like a thief in the night." In one of the books of Thessalonians, Paul says that the second coming of Christ will be like a thief in the night. Mrs. Coulter also says her love is like a "mustard seed." In one of Jesus' famous proclamations, he says that if you have faith as small as a mustard seed, you could say to a mountain, go jump in the sea, and it would do it.

This use of scripture suits Mrs. Coulter's

Mrs. Coulter's name fits the work of the Gobblers. A coulter is a blade, from the Latin *culter,* meaning "knife."

background in the Magisterium, and it points to a delicious irony in her transformation. Lyra, who causes the change and becomes the object of Mrs. Coulter's love, is the result of exactly what frightens the Magisterium most: the passionate, convention-shattering love between Mrs. Coulter and Lord Asriel. Despite Mrs. Coulter's lifelong devotion to the church and its ideals, she's finally fulfilled when she embraces the girl the Magisterium considers the Daughter of Sin.

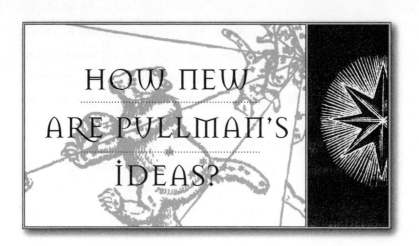

HOW NEW ARE PULLMAN'S IDEAS?

Though John Milton and William Blake are key inspirations for Pullman, a core idea in *His Dark Materials* goes back much further. As Pullman knew when he put the rebel angels on the side of good and turned God into a figure who should be overthrown, he was connecting his story to a tradition that goes back thousands of years.

Although Gnosticism is usually described as an ancient religion, and written about in the past tense, it's still practiced.

I'VE GOT A SECRET

Gnosticism (pronounced with a silent "G") is a religion that flourished during Christianity's first two centuries. Its name comes from the Greek word *gnosis*, meaning "knowledge." Like many ancient religions and some modern ones, it offered to reveal secret knowledge of spiritual truth to a select few.

In *The Golden Compass,* at the party in Mrs. Coulter's home, Lyra hears someone mention "the Zoroastrian heresy" (p. 96). Zoroastrianism is an ancient Persian religion—still practiced today—that says good and evil are equal and opposite forces. Gnosticism has a similar dualism. Mainstream Christianity does not recognize dualism, because all things are said to come from the one Creator.

Gnosticism has several branches, but one idea is common to all: The world we see is not the true world. Reality, in the Gnostic world, is actually in the spirit realm. Our bodies are false, and only our spirits are real. The material world was created to fool us.

Gnostics believe the heavenly con man is an archangel spirit called the "demiurge," from an ancient Greek word meaning "craftsman." This demiurge, they say, is the God of the Old Testament. According to Gnosticism, "He" is lying in the Bible when he claims to be the true Creator of all things and the ultimate authority in the universe. And only through Gnosticism will we gain the secret knowledge that allows us to see the real world and save our souls.

The aim of Gnosticism, then, is a reunion with the true spirit reality rather than this fake material world we know.

As many scholars have noted, this idea is similar to Plato's notion that what lies beyond our material world is an ideal world—what has been termed a "Platonic heaven." (See "Where Angels Fear to Tread," page 88.) Gnosticism's roots, though not perfectly documented, clearly go back to pre-Christian philosophies and religions. Gnosticism, however, includes Christian elements. Christ, according to Gnosticism, appeared on earth to teach humans how to reconnect to the spirit world.

Brothers in Arms

From the start, there was conflict between Gnostics and mainstream Christians. To the early Christian church, Gnosticism was a frightening double whammy: it was a rival new religion that included a role for Jesus, and it retained from old religions a touch of fascinating magic.

If you think that conflict is all in the past, think again. You can find a wide variety of descriptions of Gnosticism, but few are as colorful as the tirade, spiced with a little anti-Semitism, in the *Catholic Encyclopedia*:

As Christianity grew within and without the Roman Empire, Gnosticism spread as a fungus at its root, and claimed to be the only true form of Christianity, unfit, indeed, for the vulgar crowd, but set apart for the gifted and the elect. So rank was its poisonous growth that there seemed danger of its stifling Christianity altogether, and the earliest Fathers devoted their energies to uprooting it. Though in reality the spirit of Gnosticism is utterly alien

Teukros Basilides, Lord Asriel's alethiometer reader, gets his last name from a Gnostic who lived in Egypt in the second century. The psychologist Carl Jung wrote a book, *Seven Sermons of the Dead*, that he said came to him from the spirit of Basilides of Alexandria, with Jung only transcribing the text.

And the first name? Teukros is the name of a soldier in Homer's *Iliad*, which Pullman used to teach.

WHERE ANGELS FEAR TO TREAD

Lyra has her alethiometer; Mary Malone, in our world, makes contact with "shadows" by using a computer. She and the other researchers call the computer "the Cave." As she tries to explain to Lyra: "Shadows on the wall of the Cave, you see, from Plato." (*The Subtle Knife*, 88) But Lyra doesn't understand. She's never studied Plato.

Mary is asking a lot of Lyra, who is only twelve, but for more than a thousand years, older students have studied Plato's story about shadows in a cave. The philosopher Alfred North Whitehead joked that all of European philosophy "consists of a series of footnotes to Plato."

ME AND MY SHADOW

The dialogue about the cave, from Plato's book *The Republic*, is often the first bit of Plato that students learn, because it explains one of the foundations of Plato's philosophy, and one of its most influential ideas.

According to Plato, our senses perceive only "Forms," shadows of an ideal spiritual world that exists beyond what we can see, hear, taste, touch, and smell. Our senses give us only a rough idea of the real thing, the way a shadow shows only the outline of the object casting it.

He explained this in *The Republic* by describing a cave in which prisoners, who are chained and cannot move their heads, are looking at a cave wall that shows the shadows of people walking behind them. They see only the shadows, and assume the shadows are the actual living creatures. In Plato's explanation, that's the only reality they know. So a prisoner who's taken up to the sunlight won't believe what he sees. And if he goes back to tell the other prisoners, they won't believe him. It's too different from what they already know. They'll say he has become blind, or lost his mind, and that no one else should leave the cave.

The limitations of the prisoners describe the limitations of all of us, according to Plato. We're all in the cave.

The point of the story, Plato says, is to show that even when we think we're seeing evidence of universal ideas like Good or Justice, we're actually seeing shadows. He believed we couldn't look in our own world for those ideals, because our world is always imperfect. He believed we have to keep trying to look beyond the shadows to the true Forms, which are universal and timeless.

These Forms, says Plato, are seen "last of all" and "only with an effort." But, he adds, the effort is worthwhile, because the Forms are "the immediate source of reason and truth." A person who wants to act thoughtfully "must have his eye fixed" on this goal.

That's just what Mary and her colleagues are working on. They're trying to interpret the "shadow" particles, so they can understand the true Forms behind the shadows. Perhaps the lighthearted colleague who named the computer guessed that they'd find something unbelievable, as Plato predicted. How right he was.

A final observation: Pullman's interest in Plato is shared by mainstream religious thinkers. Plato's ideas about fixed, eternal truths that come from a higher power are related to the religious notion of Natural Law—a code of conduct from God that's more important than anything humankind could devise. Plato's ideal world is taken as a description of heaven; it's even referred to as

"Platonic heaven." After death, Plato believed, our souls are reunited with the true forms.

C. S. Lewis, the Christian author whose *Chronicles of Narnia* are so distasteful to Pullman, emphasized Plato and the story of the shadows in the cave at the end of the *Chronicles*. It's revealed that the Britain that exists in our material world is actually part of the "shadowlands," and there's an ideal form of Britain in heaven. As one character mutters, "It's all in Plato, all in Plato. . . ." (C. S. Lewis, *The Last Battle*, chapter 15)

From Plato's Republic

And now I will describe in a figure the enlightenment or unenlightenment of our nature: Imagine human beings living in an underground den which is open towards the light; they have been there from childhood, having their necks and legs chained, and can only see into the den. At a distance there is a fire, and between the fire and the prisoners a raised way, and a low wall is built along the way, like the screen over which marionette players show their puppets. Behind the wall appear moving figures, who hold in their hands various works of art, and among them images of men and animals, wood and stone, and some of the passers-by are talking and others silent.

"A strange parable," he said, "and strange captives."

They are ourselves, I replied; and they see only the shadows of the images which the fire throws on the wall of the den. To these they give names, and if we add an echo which returns from the wall, the voices of the passengers will seem to proceed from the shadows.

Suppose now that you suddenly turn them round and make them look with pain and grief to themselves at the real images; will they believe them to be real? Will not their eyes be dazzled, and will they not try to get away from the light to something which they are able to behold without blinking?

And suppose further, that they are dragged up a steep and rugged ascent into the presence of the sun himself, will not their sight be darkened with the excess of light?

Some time will pass before they get the habit of perceiving at all. At first they will be able to perceive only shadows and reflections in the water; then they will recognize the moon and the stars, and will at length behold the sun in his own proper place as he is.

Last of all they will conclude: This is he who gives us the year and the seasons, and is the author of all that we see. How will they rejoice in passing from darkness to light! How worthless to them will seem the honors and glories of the den!

But now imagine further, that they descend into their old habitations. In that underground dwelling they will not see as well as their fellows, and will not be able to compete with them in the measurement of the shadows on the wall. There will be many jokes about the man who went on a visit to the sun and lost his eyes, and if they find anybody trying to set free and enlighten one of their number, they will put him to death, if they can catch him.

Now [in this allegory] the cave or den is the world of sight, the fire is the sun, the way upwards is the way to knowledge, and in the world of knowledge the idea of good is last seen and with difficulty, but when seen is inferred to be the author of good and right—parent of the lord of light in this world, and of truth and understanding in the other.

He who attains to the beatific vision is always going upwards. He is unwilling to descend into political assemblies and courts of law, for his eyes are apt to blink at the images or shadows of images which they behold in them. He cannot enter into the ideas of those who have never in their lives understood the relation of the shadow to the substance.

But blindness is of two kinds, and may be caused either by passing out of darkness into light or out of light into darkness. A man of sense will distinguish between them, and will not laugh equally at both of them. The blindness which arises from fullness of light he will deem blessed, and pity the other. Or if he laugh at the puzzled soul looking at the sun, he will have more reason to laugh than the inhabitants of the den at those who descend from above.

There is a further lesson taught by this parable of ours. Some persons fancy that instruction is like giving eyes to the blind. But we say that the faculty of sight was always there, and that the soul only requires to be turned round towards the light.

to that of Christianity, it then seemed to the unwary merely a modification or refinement thereof. . . . Magic is the original sin of Gnosticism, nor is it difficult to guess whence it is inherited. To a certain extent it formed part of every pagan religion, especially the ancient mysteries, yet the thousands of magic tablets unearthed in Assyria and Babylonia show us where the rankest growth of magic was to be found. Moreover, the terms and names of earliest Gnosticism bear an unmistakable similarity to Semitic sounds and words. Gnosticism came early into contact with Judaism, and it betrays a knowledge of the Old Testament, if only to reject it or borrow a few names from it.

If you're wondering how the early Christians went about "uprooting" Gnosticism, that's a nice way to say Gnostics were killed.

QUESTION AUTHORITY

The Authority in *His Dark Materials* is Pullman's own version of the Gnostic demiurge: not the true Creator, but merely an archangel who takes credit for Creation. The rebel angels who fight the Authority in *His Dark Materials* are also part of the Gnostic sys-

Until very recently, most of what scholars knew about Gnosticism came secondhand, from Christian descriptions. Almost no genuine Gnostic texts existed. A 1945 discovery of ancient texts in Egypt is now the most important source of information about Gnosticism.

tem, which describes rebel angels who battle the demiurge. (See "Who Gave Daemons to Humankind?" page 97.) And, of course, the decision by Lyra and Will to choose knowledge over obedience is exactly the choice that Gnosticism requires.

So how did these Gnostic ideas get into *His Dark Materials*? Is Pullman a Gnostic?

In a word: no. However, his beliefs are certainly influenced by it. William Blake's beliefs have a lot in common with Gnosticism, and there's more than a touch of Gnosticism in John Milton's *Paradise Lost*.

Less known, but no less important to Pullman, is the novelist David Lindsay (1878–1945), author of a fantasy called *A Voyage to Arcturus* (1920). Pullman himself explains that the story, about a trip to another planet, is

> a variety of the Gnostic myth, the idea that this material world is the creation of a false god, and that it's the duty of the Gnostics, the knowing ones, to escape from the false deluding beauty of the physical universe and find their way back to the inconceivably distant true god who is their home.

Lindsay's novel, says Pullman, is "crude, badly

Philip K. Dick, whose stories have been made into popular movies like *Blade Runner* and *Total Recall*, often explored Gnostic themes. His main characters learn that what they think is the real world is actually artificial and evil. The *Matrix* films explore the same Gnostic idea.

written, ignorant and clumsy in every literary way, and yet is a work of genius." The ideas in the book are what make Pullman so passionate about it. "I can't begin to convey to you the power of Lindsay's vision," he says. "I found it overwhelming when I first read the book, thirty years ago, and I've seldom seen its equal outside Blake."

But there's a catch. "I don't agree with it," he adds. As he explains,

> I think the Gnostic vision is mistaken, in fact in some ways I think it verges on paranoia. But it's undeniably saying something serious, it's intensely and passionately questioning about the ultimate concerns of human life. Tolkien, by contrast, didn't question anything: it didn't occur to him to do so, because for him, as a Catholic, all the big questions were settled. The Church had all the answers, and that was that. Is there any doubt anywhere in *The Lord of the Rings*, even for a fraction of a second, about what is good and what is evil, what is to be praised and what is to be condemned? Not a flicker.

Pullman admits that Gnosticism is "a fascinating and very powerful and persuasive system

The first edition of *A Voyage to Arcturus* sold fewer than six hundred copies, but it was rediscovered and has been reissued often, becoming widely known and influential among authors and fantasy fiction readers.

of thought." He has drawn a lot from it. But in the end *His Dark Materials* expresses his own beliefs, which are exactly the opposite of Gnosticism's basic principle. As Pullman says, "The essence of Gnosticism is its rejection of the physical universe and the whole tendency of my thinking and feeling and of the story I wrote is towards the celebration of the physical world."

"There is one thing worse than pain, and that is pleasure."
—From David Lindsay's *Sketch Notes for a New System of Philosophy*

WHO GAVE DAEMONS TO HUMANKIND?

The novelist Michael Chabon says "the goddess of writers was smiling on Philip Pullman on the day he came up with the idea for daemons." The appeal of daemons seems to be universal. But as Pullman has revealed, his inspiration wasn't all divine. There were worldly sources.

How are daemons born? Pullman says he hasn't yet imagined that detail.

DONKEY'S EARS

One general inspiration for daemons, Pullman explains, is "the old idea of the guardian angel." Old idea is right. Stories about guardian spirits have been a part of most cultures throughout history. But as a source for Pullman, one of those guardian spirits stands out.

The Greek philosopher Socrates described a companion spirit, a "daimon," who inspired him to seek the truth and to do the right thing when a complicated situation appeared. Socrates' student Plato developed this idea further. In time it made its way into the culture of ancient Rome, where a person's guiding spirit became known as his "genius."

"I found it a very fruitful metaphor," Pullman says of Socrates' daimon. Pullman says that in his own version of the idea, "the daemon is the part of you that helps you grow towards wisdom."

WISE AS AN OWL

Though Socrates' daimon wasn't an animal, animal spirit companions have a long tradition. Norse legends, for example, describe spirits very much like Pullman's daemons. Folklorist Sabine Baring-Gould writes, "The Norsemen believed that every man had his *fylgja*, follower, a spirit intimately related to him, and that died when he did." A fylgja isn't always visible like Pullman's daemons. It reveals itself at important moments. But as Baring-Gould explains, when the fylgja does appear, it's likely to be in the shape of "any beast which represented the character or temperament of the man it followed. Brave men had companion spirits in the shape of bears or

Witches and wizards are often said to have "familiars," animal companions that are intelligent and may have magical powers. Black cats, for example, are common familiars for European witches.

wolves. That of a crafty man appeared as a fox. A timorous man had a *fylgja* in the form of a hare or a small bird." Fylgur (the plural form) were wise counselors because they could leave their humans and jump into the future. Seeing what might happen allowed them to return with good advice.

A GIFT HORSE

By coincidence, Michael Chabon was on the right track when he remarked that daemons were given to Pullman by a goddess. Though Pullman didn't mention it in *His Dark Materials*, he imagined that a goddess figure in Lyra's world gave daemons to humankind as a gift.

In *The Book of Dust*, which he's currently writing and which will reveal more of the origins of Lyra's world, Pullman plans to explain this origin for daemons, starting with the idea of rebel angels. The angels in his story, like the angels in Gnostic legends, come together to do battle with one of their kind who claims to be the original Creator of the universe. As in Gnostic myth, Pullman's rebel angels are led by a female figure, Sophia. Her name means "wisdom," and that's what she wants humankind to have. Pullman explains how he combined

"People don't always like what their daemons become. The daemon can show you things that you may not like about yourself."

— Anna Maxwell Martin, who played Lyra in the 2004 National Theatre production of *His Dark Materials*

his invention of daemons with this Gnostic idea:

Jung's term for the predominant psychological traits of men was "animus" (Latin for "soul"). Jung believed men have inner female traits— called "anima," from the feminine form of the same Latin word—if they're psychologically balanced. A balanced woman has a dominant anima but also a male animus.

The rebel angels led by Sophia gave to the beings in each world who were evolving, a gift that would help them understand themselves and become wise. In some worlds, they gave them a daemon. In other worlds, they gave them a song that could pull down wisdom from the stars. In a world which we visit in the course of *The Amber Spyglass*, they gave them the gift of riding on wheels. . . . But in each case you see this gift is to help one achieve wisdom . . . which is the sort of natural status of life and consciousness, towards which we move almost gravitationally.

A MAN'S BEST FRIEND

Connected to that idea of growth and wisdom is Pullman's rule that a daemon is generally the opposite gender of its human counterpart. Pullman explains, "If I had a spirit companion, if you'd like to call it [that], I would like to think that it was the opposite sex because there's a completeness about the relationship between [the] two sexes in that way."

Pullman didn't borrow this idea. It occurred

to him for the same reason it's occurred to others: it's as natural a unity as can be imagined. It's been the subject of many psychological theories, most notably by psychologist Carl Jung (1875–1961), who said everyone's psyche includes qualities of the opposite gender. William Blake had his own view of this dual aspect of personality. He imagined that sometimes people were unnaturally separated from their opposite sides. The separated part of the psyche then became what Blake called an "emanation." Eve was an emanation of Adam, in Blake's view. She was created when the female side of Adam's persona separated from him. Blake believed it was natural for these opposites to come together.

Pullman has said some people have daemons of the same gender, which is "a rather unusual gift." Like the relationship of the angels Baruch and Balthamos, which is presented with no explanation and raises no questions in the minds of other characters, same-sex daemons can be taken as Pullman's statement that homosexuality is perfectly natural.

Clever As a Fox

There's no doubt that Pullman's creation of daemons is a case of artistic inspiration. That said, daemons are also a clever storytelling device. Talking animals are always an attention-grabber. More than that, by giving Lyra a talking companion that's actually a part of her, Pullman is able to leave her as a solitary hero while still creating conflict between characters. From the moment we meet Lyra and Pan in the Retiring Room, they're arguing. It seems they don't stop for the next 1,400 pages. The

THE PANTALAIMON CODE

Who could have guessed Pantalaimon's final form? He only becomes a pine marten once, at the end. Why didn't Pullman choose a lion to show Lyra's courage, or a bear for her strong will, or a raven for her tricky, "Silvertongue" ways?

Well, the final choice wasn't a complete surprise. There are clues in *His Dark Materials*. But Pullman says it was partly a whimsical choice. It also makes sense when you learn what inspired it.

MONA LISA SMILE

The form that seems to please Pan the most is an ermine, which is similar to a pine marten but not quite the same. (They're from the same animal family, weasels, but pine martens are larger.) Early in *The Golden Compass* Pullman tells us it's Pan's "favorite sleeping form" (page 27), and later simply Pan's "favorite" even when he's awake (page 217). "I loved that sinuous shape," Pullman has explained.

But what first brought an ermine to mind? A childhood pet? A favorite animal from literature? No, something less obvious. An image in a painting by Leonardo da Vinci.

Because of the painting's strange history—for a long

time it was moved from place to place to avoid being stolen in wartime—it's not as well known as works like his *Mona Lisa*. However, it's considered among his greatest.

It has become known as simply *Lady with an Ermine*.

For hundreds of years, the lady's identity was uncertain. There were a few possibilities. Scholars have now decided she is Cecilia Gallerani, a young Italian woman who was the lover of a duke in Milan.

They aren't quite sure precisely why she is holding an ermine. One theory is her name is similar to the ancient Greek word for ermine, *galeē*. More likely, it was meant to be a symbol of her lover. The ermine was the duke's emblem. Throwing off all these theories is the claim by some people that the painting should never have been titled *Lady with an Ermine*. They say the animal is clearly a ferret!

The relationship between the lady and the ermine is what

Lady with an Ermine, Leonardo da Vinci, circa 1490.

Pullman noticed. It brought Pan to life for him. "There's a real connection between the girl and the animal," he explains. "That is her daemon. And while she is dressed much more elegantly than Lyra would be, if you made a few small alterations, yes, she could be Lyra."

PANDAEMONIUM

Why, then, doesn't Pan simply settle into an ermine form?

Pullman knew that "ermine" is the name given to a short-tailed weasel – a stoat – during winter, when its coat becomes white so it can hide in the snow. If Pan settled into ermine form, he'd be a stoat part of every year. Names like "stoat" and "weasel," Pullman says, "just didn't fit the animal I had in mind." In *His Dark Materials*, Pan becomes a stoat only once: when Will first encounters Pan and Lyra, Pan changes from a "large wildcat" to a "red-brown stoat with a cream throat and belly." (*The Subtle Knife*, 20) But something close to stoat was the right choice. "The pine marten is essentially the same shape," Pullman explains, "and its fur is a beautiful chestnut brown color."

So at the end of *His Dark Materials* Pan settles into essentially the same form that inspired Pullman at the beginning, and the intimate relationship captured by Leonardo da Vinci more than five hundred years ago lives on.

WHAT'S IN A NAME?

Is there a work of art behind Pan's extraordinary name? Or, as one scholar wondered, did it come from Saint Pantaleon, a rebellious cleric who, according to legend, cheated five executioners before finally succumbing?

No. Pullman says,

Much as I'd like to pretend to have a profound reason for everything I do, I have to say that in this case Pantalaimon was just the name that came to my mind. It sounded right in the same way that Lyra sounded right.

PLENTY OF MOXIE

Will Parry doesn't have an animal daemon—as Lyra deduces, he has something inside him that serves the same purpose—but he does have a cat, Moxie. And Moxie is also a guide. She's the one who discovers the opening from Will's world into the parallel world of Cittàgazze.

So is it significant that Moxie is a cat, the way it's significant that in Lyra's world a daemon's form means something?

Yes, but it's not a comment about Will, and the allusion is more playful than anything else. Pullman's notions about parallel worlds are based in part on real science, especially ideas developed from quantum physics. There happens to be a story about a cat connected to the development of quantum theory.

Without going into scientific detail, let's just say quantum theory arose from the problem scientists had when devising equations to describe how light moves. Sometimes light seems to behave like a wave, sometimes like a tiny particle. In the 1920s, a few scientists began to wonder if it could be both. Interesting equations developed

quickly. But they didn't solve all the theoretical problems.

In 1935 Erwin Schrödinger, a Nobel Prize–winning quantum physicist, challenged his colleagues by describing a hypothetical experiment that would show the limits of the equations that existed at the time. He said that if you put a cat in a box with a particular device that could kill the cat under one circumstance but not another, quantum theory would show that inside the box you'd have an animal that was a mixture of live cat and dead cat. Obviously, that can't be.

"Schrödinger's cat" has been the basis for a lot of theories that followed, including theories about multiple worlds. *The Science of Philip Pullman's "His Dark Materials,"* an excellent book by Mary and John Gribbin, is the place to learn more about this subject. The Gribbins have also written *In Search of Schrödinger's Cat: Quantum Physics and Reality* and *Schrödinger's Kittens and the Search for Reality: Solving the Quantum Mysteries.*

back-and-forth between Lyra and Pan reveals Lyra's deepest thoughts and drives the story forward. Without Pan, we might grow tired of Lyra debating with herself before every action. "Do I leave the wardrobe? Do I stay?" Too much of that would seem like indecision, and she wouldn't be an exciting hero.

This isn't to say Pullman was calculating when he invented daemons. But you can be sure he recognized their storytelling value very quickly. You can also be sure he understands the deepest reason for their appeal. They're not about loving another creature; they're about loving oneself. The question Pullman's readers ask so often—"What sort of daemons would I have?"—is really no different from "Who am I?" Even Lyra ponders that question of identity, because she has to wonder about Pan's final form.

That idea of a changing daemon—entirely Pullman's—is another storytelling hook. We never know what form Pan will take next. But it's much more than a special effect. It's connected to a central theme of the story. Pullman explained to scholars Wendy Parsons and Catriona Nicholson how it came to him:

Well, this is something that came after a great deal of sitting and groaning. I couldn't get the story going at all. I didn't have daemons to start with, but I had Lyra and I had the shape of the story, and I had a lot of incidents for the first book. However, I couldn't get it going. It didn't work, and it wouldn't work, until after one of these days of sitting and groaning and wishing, I wrote the words "Lyra and her daemon," and then I realized I didn't know why she'd have a daemon, or what her daemon was, but thought it sounded intriguing, and so I wrote the rest of that chapter. Then I knew I was on the verge of something. In the first draft, as I wrote it down, everybody's daemon changed form; adults' as well, so when Lyra is hiding in the cupboard and the servant comes in, his daemon changed shape. I wrote the first chapter pretty well exactly the same except for this, and then I stopped and I realized . . . and I almost got excited, very excited, but I hadn't quite got it yet. . . . It was merely picturesque. This was a world where everybody had a daemon that changed shape. So what? But then I thought and thought and related it to what I now knew was the theme of the book, namely the change from innocence to experience, and it suddenly came to

An alert fan once asked Pullman how Will could see Pan right away if you have to learn to see daemons. Pullman's amusing reply: "That is a very good question. That's one of the best questions I've heard for a long time. In fact it's such a good question that any answer I could give would be insufficient to match the profundity and complexity of the issues you raise. I shall have to confess my ignorance and tiptoe away."

me, of course, that children's daemons could change, but then when they, as it were, Fall, they become mature and settle down in one fixed form. That was the point when I knew I'd got the whole thing. I knew I could use this to say something about the theme. The difference between adulthood and childhood could be signified by their daemons. It was the most exciting moment I've ever had in writing.

A dramatic moment with a dazzling result—but more than that too. As Pullman's story reveals, the notion of changing daemons only appeared to come to him as a flash of insight. He had to work toward it. And that as much as anything else shows what daemons are about. Describing changing daemons, he once said,

> I found that a very good way of demonstrating the difference between children and grown-ups . . . the sort of infinite potentiality children have, the great malleability of their characters. They change very quickly, their moods change. Grown-ups don't have that. We've lost that. But on the other hand, we've gained some-

Pullman says his daemon would probably be a magpie, because magpies like to pick up shiny things and Pullman likes to grab things out of the books he reads.

thing as well. We've gained a sort of subtle strength, a singleness of purpose which will carry us through to the destination which we're aiming for. I suppose you could say if children have innocence and then we lose that innocence, what we can hope to gain by living and suffering and working and loving and losing is wisdom. And the great difference is that innocence can't be wise, but wisdom can't be innocent. That, of course, is the underpinning of the whole story.

Though Pullman is talking about the underpinning of the story's themes, it turns out that he crafted the story itself the same way.

Pullman has also said his daemon could be a raven, like the trickster spirit in Native North American legends, because tricksters tell stories.

I Need That Like I Need a Hole in the Head

If you hadn't heard of trepanning before reading *His Dark Materials*, you probably assumed Pullman invented it. But it's real.

It wasn't just a bizarre ritual of an isolated group. It was practiced on many continents. Trepanned skulls have been found from Russia to Peru, and even on the banks of the Thames River in London. Many four- and five-thousand-year-old skulls show evidence of trepanning. Other examples appear to be much older—perhaps ten thousand years or more.

Strangest of all: the practice continues today.

In case you're wondering, surgeons only discovered good painkillers about one hundred and fifty years ago. But it seems that there's less pain in brain surgery than you'd imagine, so painkillers weren't necessary. Still, it's not something you'd expect people to enjoy. After the skin was cut and pulled back, the holes could be scraped with a sharp knife or cut with a stone or blade. Sophisticated drill bits were used by the "advanced" surgeons of the nineteenth century.

There are many examples of skulls with more than one trepanning hole. At least one example has five holes, all made at different times.

This brings up an important point. Most people survived trepanning. Two out of three trepanned skulls show bone growing back. And of the other one out of three, there's evidence that some of the "patients" were dead before the procedure began. Those who did die were usually killed by infection, not bleeding.

Keep an Open Mind

So why would anyone want a hole in the head? (Or two, or five?) Scientists have several theories. There are certainly examples where a surgeon was releasing pressure on the brain caused by a wound, much as surgeons do today. It's also possible that trephination (another term for trepanning) was used as therapy for mental illness or epilepsy. Some cultures may have believed that evil spirits had to be released. Others may have believed the holes were ways for spirits to enter.

Brainpower

No skulls have been dated as far back as Lyra's alethiometer says: thirty-three thousand years ago. That's an invention of Pullman's. But it wasn't chosen casually. You may have noticed that a colleague of Mary Malone discovered "a great increase in the number of shadow particles [Dust]" about that time. "Something had happened then," she thinks to herself, "some development in evolution." (*The Amber Spyglass*, page 223) The mulefa, she discovers, also trace their history back thirty-three thousand years.

Why did Pullman choose that figure? The answer lies in our world. For reasons archaeologists can't yet explain, there's evidence for a leap forward in human culture about thirty-three thousand years ago. Early humans suddenly started to produce small works of art—stone figurines, for example. These aren't crude works. "These people knew exactly what they were doing and they were very good at it," says Nicholas Conard, a paleo-anthropologist at the University of Tübingen in Germany. "There does appear to be quite a different life before and after," adds Anthony Sinclair, an archaeologist at the University of Liverpool in England.

For Pullman, the creation of art—a sign of trying to understand the world, and to tell stories about humankind's place in it, is the date at which human consciousness began. In *His Dark Materials*, that process began with the arrival of Dust.

WHO TRIED TO INVENT A REAL ALETHIOMETER?

In *The Golden Compass*, Lyra learns a little of the alethiometer's history from Dr. Lanselius, the witches' Consul at Trollesund. He says that in the seventeenth century, a scholar in Prague wanted "a way of measuring the influences of the planets, according to the ideas of astrology." The symbols were part of the language of that time. "Buildings [with carved images] and pictures were designed to be read like books," Lanselius says. (*The Golden Compass*, 173)

On the website of his American publisher, Random House, Pullman offers more of this imaginary history. His explanation sounds so believable that you might think it's real. In fact Pullman is just having fun, extending his novel's backstory. But some of what he created

Alethia is a Latin word meaning "truth," so an alethiometer is an instrument that measures truth.

is based on real history he had in mind when he imagined the device. And though none of the scholars he mentions ever tried to build a machine exactly like Lyra's, they did try to gain the knowledge it offers. Some of their methods would look familiar to Lyra.

ONE MAGIC MOMENT

In his invented history, Pullman says, "The first alethiometer was constructed in Prague during the reign of Rudolf II by a scholar named Pavel Khunrath." At the time, Pullman says, Prague was "a hotbed of alchemy."

That bit of fictional history is based on fact. A real Rudolf II reigned over the Holy Roman Empire from 1576 to 1612. He was a great supporter of alchemy. This may seem ridiculous now, but at the time alchemists were considered serious scholars, and some of what they learned became the basis for modern chemistry. Because Rudolf hired alchemists from all over the world to work in Prague, the city was known as the Metropolis of Alchemy.

One of the best known alchemists of the time was indeed named Khunrath—but *Heinrich* Kunrath, not Pavel. The name change is Pullman's signal that he's fictionalizing history, not following it.

Despite the connections in contemporary literature between alchemy and witchcraft, Christianity was not originally opposed to alchemy. Many religious figures, including St. Thomas Aquinas, dabbled in it.

The details of Heinrich Khunrath's life are sketchy. Apparently he was born about 1560 in Germany, and educated at the University of Basel, Switzerland. He chose not to focus on making gold, but rather on using alchemy to make contact with divine wisdom. This spiritual style of alchemy, called Hermeticism, was widespread during the Renaissance. Based on the study of texts that appeared to come from ancient Egypt and therefore were considered the source of powerful ancient wisdom, Hermeticism combined magic, Christianity, and a branch of Jewish mysticism. (The texts, it was later discovered, dated from the first centuries of Christianity.) They were similar to Gnostics in thinking that the spiritual goal of humankind should be to become unified with the divine world.

Just as Lyra's ability read truths from the alethiometer seems to come from supernatural grace, Khunrath tried to develop a system that would magically reveal eternal and divine truths. He organized his studies visually to show the relationships between branches of knowledge. His circular designs, which appear in his book *Theater of Eternal Wisdom* (*Amphitheatrum Sapientiae Aeternae*; 1595), suggest the alethiometer. They're similar to symbol-filled circles in many Hermetic texts.

Hermeticism gets its name because its main texts are written as dialogue with the god Hermes Trismegistus ("Thrice-great Hermes"), the Greek version of Thoth, god of magic and knowledge. Many Hermeticists believed Hermes Trismegistus was the actual author of the magical instructions in the texts.

POSITIVELY NEGATIVE

In *The Subtle Knife*, when Mary Malone explains to Lyra how to speak with the "shadow particles," she mentions a nineteenth-century Romantic poet, John Keats. It's more than a passing reference. Pullman brings in Keats throughout *His Dark Materials*: when Giacomo Paradisi is trying to teach Will how to use the knife; when Mary Malone creates the Amber Spyglass; and then when Will and Lyra, in the mulefa's world, sense "shadows" are nearby.

Pullman isn't referring to a poem by Keats, but instead to an idea Keats mentioned in a letter. Held up as an example of Romantic thinking, it's known by the same term Mary Malone uses: "negative capability."

As Mary quotes to Lyra from a note she keeps on her desk, people who want to speak with the "dark particles" – which we soon learn are angels – must be "capable of being in uncertainties, mysteries, doubts, without any irritable reaching after fact and reason." Or as scholar Millicent Lenz puts it, negative capability allows you to "live creatively with contradictions, to transcend the dualism of good and evil."

Here is the text of Keats's original letter:

Hampstead Sunday   *[December 21, 1817]*

MY DEAR BROTHERS,

. . . I spent Friday evening with Wells, and went next morning to see [the recently completed Benjamin West painting] "Death on the Pale Horse." It is a wonderful picture, when West's age is considered [West was 79; Keats was 23]; But there is nothing to be intense upon; no woman one feels mad to kiss, no face swelling into reality—The excellence of every art is its intensity, capable of making all disagreeables evaporate, from their being in close relationship with Beauty and Truth. . . .

I dined with Haydon the Sunday after you left, and had a very pleasant day, I dined too (for I have been out too much lately) with Horace Smith, and met his two Brothers, with Hill and Kingston, and one Du Bois. They only served to convince me, how superior humour is to wit in respect to enjoyment—These men say things which make one start [startle], without making one feel; they are all alike; their manners are alike; they all know fashionables; they have a mannerism in their eating and drinking, in their mere handling a Decanter—They talked of Kean and his low company [bad friends]—Would I were with that Company instead of yours, said I to myself! . . . I had not a dispute but a disquisition, with Dilke on various subjects; several things dovetailed in my mind, and at once it struck me what quality went to form a Man of Achievement, especially in Literature, and which Shakespeare possessed so enormously—I mean Negative Capability, that is, when a man is capable of being in uncertainties, mysteries, doubts, without any irritable reaching after fact and reason. . . .

Pullman's fictional Khunrath investigated what Pullman calls "the memory-theater system of symbolic images." That's a real idea that did interest the real Heinrich Khunrath. It's an ancient idea that had come back into style in Khunrath's time. The foundation for it is simply a trick many people still use to remember things: they associate the thing to be remembered—a name, for example—with a single, simple image. Then they just worry about remembering the image. The details come back when needed. As an additional memory trick, these symbols could be imagined as objects within a house. So you can remember all sorts of complex things by remembering something as familiar as your own home.

Sir Isaac Newton was greatly influenced by Hermeticism.

From this came the idea of memory theater, a small auditorium in which a scholar or two could stand on the equivalent of the stage and look out at a semicircular arrangement of boxes or drawers placed where the seats would be in a normal theater. Stored within would be scrolls with texts about a specific subject.

Pullman's history of the alethiometer credits a scholar named Giulio Camillo with influencing the fictional Pavel Khunrath's interest in memory theaters. In our world, Giulio Camillo was a real scholar, born about

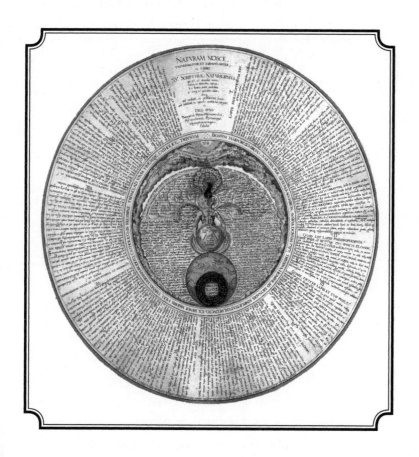

from *Amphitheatrum Sapientiae Aeternae*

from *Amphitheatrum Sapientiae Aeternae*

1460, who was very prominent in the first half of the sixteenth century. His patrons included a king of France. He devoted a lot of thought to memory theaters, and claimed to have built one. Camillo's memory theater was meant to be a collection of all human knowledge.

Not every scholar believes Camillo should be taken seriously. Some make the point that Camillo lived before printed books were common—centuries before the *Encyclopedia Britannica*, for example—so a collection of knowledge like his might seem exciting. Though libraries existed, his theater could theoretically be created anywhere. On the other hand, the whole idea could have just been a grand scheme to stay on the royal payroll.

What did become real, because of its influence on later scholars, was Camillo's interest in organizing all of human knowledge into a single system. The memory theater arranged symbols so they followed the history of human thought, which Camillo, and many others, saw as growing from a divine origin.

The arrangement of ideas in Camillo's memory theater was based on mythology and astronomy, with seven main sections for the seven planets known at the time.

MR. UNIVERSES

Giordano Bruno, also mentioned in Pullman's history, was another real scholar. Like Camillo, he was interested in memory devices. Yet his connection to Pullman's work goes far beyond

In Lyra's world, according to a brief reference in *The Golden Compass,* John Calvin became pope. This is meant as a joke. In our world, Calvin (1509–1564), was perhaps the single most influential Protestant reformer. Though he was as authoritarian as any pope—Calvinism is associated with strict rules and severe punishments—Calvin wouldn't have been welcome at the Vatican.

the alethiometer. His biography is full of similarities to *His Dark Materials.* It includes conflicts with the established church, time in Oxford, and theories about multiple worlds.

Bruno, who lived from 1548 to 1600, questioned the Catholic church from an early age, despite studying to be a priest. Soon after being ordained he was put on trial for reading forbidden pamphlets. He escaped, was falsely accused of murder, and fled Italy. Ending up in Geneva, he began to follow the ideas of John Calvin, who also challenged the Catholic church. Bruno decided Calvinism had its own faults, and made his thoughts known. The outcome was familiar: arrest, trial, excommunication, and exile to yet another country.

In France, Bruno began to study memory devices, and to explain his own view of the universe. Bruno believed that each star could be a sun with planets, and those planets could have intelligent life. He believed there are an infinite number of stars, and therefore there are an infinite number of worlds with life.

In the sixteenth century, ideas about life beyond Earth or multiple universes were shocking. Even worse: Bruno didn't think the heavens are the home of God, or that the stars are made from a different kind of matter than is found on earth. Bruno believed all matter is made from the same elements, and those elements have an energy or life force. In a way, he believed in Dust.

Bruno kept on the move, and spent time in Pullman's (and Lyra's) city, Oxford. Unfortunately, the scholars there believed none of his theories, not even the idea that the Earth revolves around the Sun. They certainly didn't agree that there's no God in the traditional sense of an all-powerful Creator. And they didn't agree that all religions can coexist.

Foolishly, Bruno returned to Italy, where the pope had him arrested and imprisoned. Finally, like Pavel Khunrath in Pullman's invented history, Bruno was burned at the stake.

There's a statue of Bruno in the center of Rome's famous Campo de' Fiori. It's on the spot where he was executed.

SPINNING YOUR WHEELS?

Pullman's "official" history of the alethiometer omits an inspiration he has revealed in interviews. It's a kind of book that was popular in the 1500s and 1600s. In these volumes, called "emblem books," a common phrase—usually one with a moral—was expressed with a picture. It was considered entertaining to decode the meaning from the symbols, though the books offered explanations.

The passion for emblem books began with the publication in Italy of Andrea Alciato's *Emblematum Liber* ("Book of Emblems") in

The Minde should have a fixed Eye
On Objects, that are plac'd on High.

ILLVSTR. XLIII.   Book. I.

A Heart, which bore the figure of an Eye
Wide open to the Sunne; by some, was us'd,
When in an Emblem, they would signifie
A Minde, which on Celestiall Matters mus'd:
Implying, by the same, that there is nought
Which in this lower Orbe, our Eyes can see,
So fit an Object for a manly thought,
As those things, which in Heav'n above us be.

From a 1635 British emblem book by George Wither: *A Collection of Emblemes, Ancient and Moderne, Quickened with metricall illustrations, both Morall and divine: And Disposed into lotteries, that instruction, and good counsell, may bee furthered by an honest and pleasant recreation.*

124

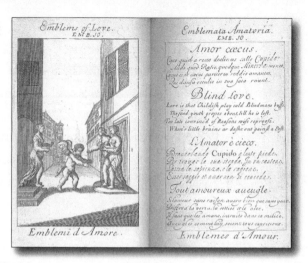

"Blind Love: Love is that Childish play called Blindman's bluff,
the fond youth gropes about till he is lost. . . . "

"Persevere: What if her heart be found as hard as flint?
What if her cruel breast be turned to oak? . . ."
from *Emblemata Amatoria*, Philip Ayres, London, 1683.

1531. Some emblem books were devoted to love; others were more intellectual. What Lanselius tells Lyra about that time in their world was also true in ours: "Symbols and emblems were everywhere." (*The Golden Compass*, 173)

Pullman says he was fascinated by this use of pictures to express ideas or information, or to "make a moral point." For the alethiometer, he combined traditional emblem book symbols with ones of his own creation.

Over the centuries, Alciato's *Emblematum Liber* has appeared in more than 150 editions in many languages.

Then, after establishing the "rules" for his invention, he had a surprise. In a library in Oxford he found a book in which, as he says, "it looked as though someone had actually drawn the alethiometer."

What Pullman found printed in the book was a spinner device like you'd use with a board game. The reader was supposed to give it a twirl while asking a question about love. The number on the spinner would direct the reader to the emblem with the answer. But unlike the alethiometer, which Lyra can read because her lack of self-consciousness gives her a nearly divine grace, readers of emblem books weren't helped by the angels. Except maybe Cupid.

The Figure or Lottery.

THis Game occasions not the frequent crime
   Of swearing, or mispending of our time,
Nor loss of money, for the Play is short,
And every Gamester winneth by the sport:
We therefore Judge, it may as well become,
The *Hall*, the Parlor, or the *Dining Room*,
As Chess or Tables; and we think the price
Will be as low, because it needs no Dice.

Several emblem books included backgrounds for spinners.
Above, the spinner is knotted in place with thread. From
Choice emblems, divine and moral, antient and modern,
by "R. B.," London, 1732.

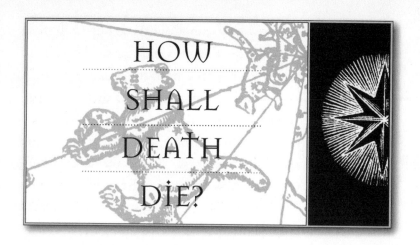

HOW SHALL DEATH DIE?

Lyra and Will's trip to the land of the dead may seem familiar to anyone who has read classic epics like *The Odyssey* and the *Aeneid.* Pullman freely borrows bits of those stories, just as each of them borrowed from earlier works. However, Pullman bends those earlier stories to his own ideas, which are influenced by his own experiences. His conclusion, his idea of death, stands as one of the greatest differences between *His Dark Materials* and mainstream thought. It's directly linked to his belief in how we should live.

Both the Greek hero Odysseus and the Roman hero Aeneas make trips to the underworld. Odysseus is directed there by the sorceress Circe. Aeneas is accompanied by the Cumaean Sybil, a priestess and prophetess.

DAY TRIPPERS

Avoiding any overly personal revelation, Pullman says his primary reason for thinking about the afterlife is "probably the same as everyone's who wonders about it: it has occupied the thoughts and fears and hopes of human beings for tens of thousands of years."

As we'll see in a moment, there may be another, more private reason in addition to this one. But for now, his remark points to something important about the epics from which he drew material, and the cultures from which they came. In many cases, a trip to the land of the dead is the core of an epic story. Literature scholar Joseph Campbell says that type of journey is required of nearly all epic heroes. Because we fear death and what comes after—or what might not—we want stories about heroes who have been to the land of the dead but were strong enough to come back to the land of the living. One example is *Gilgamesh*, which originated around four thousand years ago in what's now Iraq and which is sometimes called the world's oldest novel. In the story, the death of a friend compels Gilgamesh, a Sumerian king, to make the journey to the land of the dead. A primary theme in the story is the need for Gilgamesh to overcome his fear of death.

By design, the land of the dead in *His Dark Materials* has elements in common with afterworlds or underworlds in those ancient tales. For example, the ferryman who carries

The version of the Gilgamesh legend that has survived dates from the Babylonian era, about 2000 B.C. A real king Gilgamesh, on whom the legends were apparently based, lived about four hundred years earlier, when Sumerian culture dominated the region.

Lyra and Will to the land of the dead is like the character Charon from Greek mythology, who ferried the dead across the Rivers Styx and Acheron to the realm of Hades, god of the underworld. You may recall that early in *His Dark Materials*, Lyra finds several skulls, each with a metal disk in its mouth—a "daemon-coin, showing its owner's lifetime companion still close to him in death." (*The Golden Compass*, 50) In ancient Greece, the dead were buried with a coin in their mouths to pay Charon for the crossing.

Another similarity: Lyra and Will must argue their way into the land of the dead because, as the ferryman tells them, living beings are forbidden there. This taboo is repeated in myths from all over the world. A Babylonian story from around the time of *Gilgamesh* tells of the descent of the goddess Ishtar to "the land of no return," where she must threaten to "break the door" and "wrench the lock" before she's allowed to enter.

The flip side of this rule is that if a living person somehow gets inside, he or she will be told it's impossible to leave. In Dante Alighieri's *Divine Comedy*, a traveler to Hell encounters a man encased in flame and asks the man his name. The man hesitates, because he's ashamed to be in Hell. Then he decides to

Ishtar, the Babylonian goddess of fertility and love, was worshipped widely. She was also a god of war, and there are many legends about her cruelty. In Sumerian mythology she was known as Inanna.

respond, and explains why:

> *If I believed that my reply were made*
> *To one who to the world would e'er return,*
> *This flame without more flickering would*
> *stand still;*
> *But inasmuch as never from this depth*
> *Did any one return, if I hear true,*
> *Without the fear of infamy I answer . . .*
> (*Inferno*, Canto 27)

Psychologists have other theories to explain why the living can't visit the land of the dead. For example, it's easier to accept the separation from dead loved ones if it's imposed by a divine rule.

HERE BE MONSTERS

Because underworld stories are so common, it's almost too easy to find parallels between the classics and *His Dark Materials*. They seem to appear even where Pullman did not intend any. For example, in the Bible's Book of Matthew, Jesus Christ was said to "harrow hell" and free souls there. Considering Pullman's knowledge of the Bible, and *His Dark Material*'s many intentional connections to the Christian gospels, it's reasonable to expect Pullman had that scene in mind when Lyra freed the dead she found. But Pullman doesn't count it among his influences. "I don't know very much about it," he says. "It doesn't figure in my reading."

However, one intentional parallel is worth a closer look: Lyra's arguments with the harpies, and the deal struck with them by the Gallivespian Tialys that allows Lyra and Will to leave, are very much like a scene from one of the oldest plays in literature. This parallel is one Pullman acknowledges.

The play was written by Aeschylus (525–456 B.C.), an Athenian who's credited as the first playwright to have more than one actor on stage at a time. (Prior to that, a single actor shared the stage with a chorus that commented on the play.)

It's titled *The Eumenides*, which means "The Kindly Ones." The title is ironic. It refers to mythological creatures who are anything but kind, at least at first. They're the Erinyes—better known to us by their name in Roman mythology, the Furies. Daughters of Mother Earth, they're horrifying creatures with wings and snaky hair. Their role is to exact justice for great crimes like the murder of a relative. They usually frighten their prey to death.

Aeschylus also added some of the flash that we take for granted in plays now, such as costumes and sets.

In Aeschylus's play, they chase a man called Orestes to Athens because he has killed his mother. The goddess Athena, patron of Athens, comes to the aid of Orestes, but the Erinyes don't want to listen to her. They say they're more ancient than she is, so she must respect them.

Blake's Illustrations for Dante's Divine Comedy

Pullman's thoughts about harpies date back to his teenage years. Though he has kept the details private, he says that in his early twenties, "I saw Blake's illustrations to Dante, and felt a jolt of shocked recognition."

The illustrations, for a series that was incomplete at Blake's death, come from scenes in *Inferno*, the section of *The Divine Comedy* in which Dante described hell as a series of concentric circles of misery and pain—the worse you are in your lifetime, the closer to the frozen center you go. (Within the circles are various ditches and zones arranged according to a complex scheme that delineates one sin from the other with a precision the creators of the Global Positioning System would envy. Unfortunately, envy would condemn them to Purgatory—the Second Terrace of Purgatory, to be more specific.)

The Whirlwind of Lovers

The Baffled Devils Fighting

The Pit of Disease: The Falsifiers

The Circle of Traitors

"America: A Prophecy"

A quotation from Blake's "America: A Prophecy" (1793) appears at the beginning of *The Amber Spyglass*. "It has been very important for me for a long time, that particular passage," Pullman says. "It seemed to express very clearly what happens when the dead are finally set free." The epigraph reads:

> The morning comes,
>   the night decays, the
>   watchmen leave their
>   stations;
> The grave is burst, the spices
>   shed, the linen wrapped up;
> The bones of death, the
>   cov'ring clay, the sinews
>   shrunk & dry'd,
> Reviving shake, inspiring move,
>   breathing, awakening,
> Spring like redeemed
>   captives when their bonds
>   & bars are burst.
> Let the slave grinding at the
>   mill run out into the field:
> Let him look up into the heavens
>   & laugh in the bright air;
> Let the inchained soul shut up
>   in darkness and in sighing,
> Whose face has never seen a
>   smile in thirty weary years,
> Rise and look out; his chains
>   are loose, his dungeon
>   doors are open.
> And let his wife and
>   children return from the
>   oppressor's scourge.
> They look behind at every step
>   & believe it is a dream,
> Singing: "The Sun has
>   left his blackness, &
>   has found a fresher
>   morning
> And the fair Moon rejoices in
>   the clear & cloudless night;
> For Empire is no more, and now
>   the Lion & Wolf shall cease."

Blake's work, written after the American Revolution and during the French Revolution, used characters from Blake's invented mythology to connect political freedom with freedom from religious and psychological oppression—themes also central to *His Dark Materials*.

Athena calms them by agreeing, and suggests a settlement. Let Orestes go and stop seeking vengeance; in return, the Athenians will worship them:

The Erinyes had first names that reflected their individual characters. Roughly translated, they are Megaera ("jealous anger"), Tisiphone ("blood avenger"), and Alecto ("tireless in pursuit").

> *As time goes on, my citizens will win*
> *increasing honour, and you, on your*
> > *thrones,*
> *seated outside the house of Erechtheus* [a
> > *former king of Athens*],
> *a place of honour, will win more respect*
> *from lines of men and women filing past*
> *than you could find in all the world*
> > *beyond.*
> *So cast no stones for bloodshed on this land,*
> *my realm. Do not corrupt our youthful*
> > *hearts,*
> *intoxicating them with rage, like wine. . . .*
> *Do good things, receive good things in hon-*
> > *our.*
> *Take your place in a land the gods all love.*
> *. . . Speak nothing*
> *of brutal victories—only blessings*
> *stemming from the earth, the ocean depths,*
> *the heavens.*

"Your magic is doing its work," one of the Erinyes replies. "I feel my rage diminishing." In *His Dark Materials*, that's exactly what the harpies feel after Tialys reasons with them. And just as the Erinyes in Aeschylus's play become the Kindly Ones, the harpies in *His Dark Materials* become kind.

Building a Mystery

It's important to note that harpies, not Erinyes, are the monsters in *His Dark Materials*. One reason is classical mythology. The Erinyes are generally associated with vengeance, while harpies snatch the souls of the dead without thinking about justice. There's another reason, though for now it remains Pullman's secret. In an interview, he referred to it cryptically. Speaking about the land of the dead, he said, "Mine comes largely from classical mythology, as you can probably tell, together with some very personal things about the harpies that come out of my own mythology, going back to when I was sixteen." He may write about it someday, he said. "If I say anything now it'll fix it while it's still developing."

Whether or not he chooses to explain further, we already know something relevant about his personal mythology. He has connected a deeply personal detail of his life to themes in his work:

[Author] Peter Dickinson and I were

It was common for people to superstitiously avoid the wrath of the Erinyes by calling them the Eumenides instead. Another flattering name for them was Semnai, "venerable ones."

talking one day and this subject came up and we agreed how strange it was that so many children's authors had lost one or both parents in their childhood. My father died in a plane crash when I was seven, and naturally I was preoccupied for a long time by the mystery of what he must have been like.

That's an astute observation. Some of the most widely read authors experienced the same thing. J. R. R. Tolkien lost both his parents while he was a child. When J. K. Rowling was a young teenager, her mother was diagnosed with a fatal disease. C. S. Lewis lost his mother when he wasn't quite ten years old. All three of them wrote stories that center on the conflict between the desire to live forever and the need to accept death. Harry Potter wishes for nothing more than the return of his parents, yet he must fight against a Dark Lord whose primary goal is to cheat death in the same way. Lewis's *Chronicles of Narnia* end with all the main characters dying and going to heaven; and one of the stories is about a boy with a dying mother who has to choose between saving her life and saving the world. Tolkien said one of his most important messages is that his Elves are made unhappy by their immortality. They

Pullman's father, an officer and pilot in the Royal Air Force, died while serving in Kenya.

have to watch everything they love die. In contrast, Tolkien's humans eventually learn that death is a gift from God. While immortality may be desirable, it's unnatural, and therefore the desire must be resisted.

Pullman answers with an appropriate word of caution when asked about this personal matter. "I mistrust the biographical way of interpreting novels, as many writers do," he says, "because we know how much we simply make up for the sake of making a pretty pattern in the story." However, he says, it "may be right" to see the connection.

MIGHTY AND DEADLY?

His Dark Materials, like the books of Rowling and Lewis and Tolkien, resolves the conflict between the desire to defeat death and the need to accept it.

"Death is going to die," Lord Asriel tells Lyra in *The Golden Compass*. (*The Golden Compass*, 377) Lyra recalls that brave announcement when she's in the land of dead. It's natural to think of Asriel's statement as an echo of the last line from the well-known sonnet "Death, be not proud" by John Donne (1572–1631):

> *Death, be not proud, though some have called thee*

Peter Dickinson, though not as well known as Pullman in the United States, has written about fifty books and has won two of Britain's most prestigious literary awards, the Carnegie Medal and the Whitbread Prize, twice each.

Mighty and dreadful, for thou art not so
. . . One short sleep past, we wake eternally,
And death shall be no more; Death, thou
shalt die.

But we have to remember that Asriel is talking, not Pullman. He's not exactly the voice of reason in the story. He represents a specific point of view, and a particular set of desires. He wants a kind of immortality. Though his words may echo John Donne, Pullman doesn't necessarily agree with them. And in fact Pullman doesn't agree. Donne believed in the traditional Christian heaven: a happy, eternal afterlife, a gift from his God for a lifetime of effort and devotion on earth. Pullman doesn't. That traditional Christian view also is voiced by a ghost in the land of the dead who "look[s] like a monk" and crosses himself before making a desperate effort to argue with Lyra, whom he calls "an agent of the Evil One himself":

Donne, raised a Catholic, became an Anglican priest and served as Royal Chaplain.

> The world we lived in was a vale of corruption and tears. Nothing there could satisfy us. But the Almighty has granted us this blessed place for all eternity, this paradise, which to the fallen souls seems bleak and barren, but which the eyes of

faith see as it is, overflowing with milk and honey and resounding with the sweet hymns of angels. This is Heaven, truly. (*The Amber Spyglass*, 320–321)

Pullman's having a laugh at the monk with that speech, though he also means it as a serious comment: the monk is working very hard to maintain his delusion. The afterlife in *His Dark Materials* isn't overflowing with milk and honey. As the poet Gertrude Stein once said of her old hometown, there's no *there* there. A ghost reminds the crowd: "The good come here as well as the wicked, and all of us languish in this gloom forever, with no hope of freedom, or joy, or sleep, or rest, or peace." (*The Amber Spyglass*, 320)

For trivia buffs: Stein's hometown was Oakland, California.

That ghost decides to follow Lyra, even though it means giving up what's left of its unique personality and falling apart into Dust again. "Even if it means oblivion . . . it won't be nothing. We'll be alive again in a thousand blades of grass, and a million leaves." (*The Amber Spyglass*, 320)

That's not a belief in nothing, as some religious critics claim. In many ways it's a courageous belief. To experience life again, we have to give up our afterlife. We have to let go of our desire to stay just as we are now.

We have to let that specific arrangement of Dust fall apart. Otherwise we'll always remain ghosts. "We can get out," says Pullman, "but at the cost of recognizing that we won't last forever. If we insist on living for eternity, the cost is horrible."

Ironically, there's a way in which Pullman's belief is very Christian. Loving oneself and putting oneself first are sins in Christianity. Casting aside that sin is considered the highest form of worship. Yet the Christian afterlife promises that our individual personalities will exist for eternity. There's an element of narcissism in that belief. It's Pullman who says we're not so important to the universe, and that we're meant to be re-created in a new form. His view of the afterlife requires us to set aside self-love.

The Christian afterlife is a reward. Pullman, by comparison, is saying we should stop thinking about being rewarded. We should stop being virtuous in order to receive something in return. There's reason enough to be virtuous, to treat other people well, without it being a rule from God or a way to gain God's favor.

If we want heaven, Pullman believes, we must make it happen before we die, because we won't be sped there afterward. More than

The phrase "earth to earth, ashes to ashes, dust to dust" doesn't appear in the Bible. It's from the Church of England's *Book of Common Prayer*. Its origin is in Genesis 3:19, which reads, "dust thou art, and unto dust shalt thou return."

that, he believes we *should* make it happen. As he explained to an audience at a literary convention, just after finishing *The Amber Spyglass* but before it was published:

> There's a phrase which comes into the third book and which occurs in the last line of the third book, especially, so it does have a particular emphasis, which sums up what I mean: and the phrase is "the Republic of Heaven." We're used to the kingdom of heaven; but you can tell from the general thrust of the book that I'm of the devil's party, like Milton. And I think it's time we thought about a republic of heaven instead of the kingdom of heaven. The king is dead. That's to say I believe that the king is dead. I'm an atheist. But we need heaven nonetheless, we need all the things that heaven meant, we need joy, we need a sense of meaning and purpose in our lives, we need a connection with the universe, we need all the things that the kingdom of heaven used to promise us but failed to deliver. And, furthermore, we need it in this world where we do exist—not elsewhere, because there ain't no elsewhere. The Republic of Heaven is the notion

"[Pullman's] republic is not so different from the kingdom. But it is a realm where authority is democratised, so what were once the king's responsibilities become our own . . . . [It rejects] unquestioning obedience and uncritical subjection to a divine lord and king, for lordship and kingship belong to the past."
—David Boulton, author of *The Trouble With God: Religious Humanism and the Republic of Heaven*

which is given its full expression in the third book. The whole thing's been leading up to that.

Believing in that notion requires its own act of faith, as Will reminds Lyra when she hesitates. "You can feel this," he says. (*The Amber Spyglass*, 321) She does. Death itself doesn't die, but fear of death does.

BIBLIOGRAPHY
AND NOTES

Select Bibliography and Online Resources

Books
Blake, William, W. H. Stevenson, ed. *William Blake: Selected Poetry*. London: Penguin, 1988. (See also William Blake Archive in Online Resources below.)
Butler, Robert. *The Art of Darkness: Staging the Philip Pullman Trilogy*. London: National Theatre with Oberon Books, 2003.
————. *Darkness Illuminated: Platform Discussions on "His Dark Materials" at the National Theatre*. Philip Pullman, Nicholas Hynter, Dr. Rowan Williams, Nicholas Wright, and others in conversation with Robert Butler. London: National Theatre with Oberon Books, 2004.
Davidson, Gustav. *Dictionary of Angels: Including the Fallen Angels*. New York: Free Press, 1967.
Gribbin, Mary, and John Gribbin. *The Science of Philip Pullman's His Dark Materials*. London: Hodder, 2003.
Pullman, Philip. "Paradise Illustrated." Speech for the opening of the exhibition "Paradise Lost: the Poem and Its Illustrators," at the Wordsworth Trust, Dove Cottage, Grasmere, England, 6 July 2004. Copyright © 2004 Philip Pullman.
————. *The Golden Compass* (UK title *Northern Lights*). Published in the United States by Alfred A. Knopf, Inc., New York. Published in Great Britain by Scholastic Children's Books. Copyright © 1995 by Philip Pullman.
————. *The Subtle Knife*. Published in the United States by Alfred A. Knopf, Inc., New York. Published in Great Britain by Scholastic Children's Books. Copyright © 1997 by Philip Pullman.
————. *The Amber Spyglass*. Published in the United States by Alfred A. Knopf, Inc., New York. Published in Great Britain by Scholastic Children's Books. Copyright © 2000 by Philip Pullman.

Two books published after the completion of this one are also recommended. Oxford University Press has published an illustrated edition of John Milton's *Paradise Lost* with an introduction by Philip Pullman. Laurie Frost's *Elements: The Elements of His Dark Materials: A Guide to Philip Pullman's Trilogy* (Fell Press, 2006) is an A-Z reference with brief entries covering people, places, things and ideas.

Articles and Interviews

Fried, Kerry. "Darkness Visible: An Interview with Philip Pullman" for Amazon.com. <www.amazon.com>

Kazin, Alfred. "An Introduction to William Blake." First printed in *The Portable Blake*, Alfred Kazin, ed. New York: Viking, 1946. Copyright © 1997 Alfred Kazin. Possible online resource: <http://www.multimedialibrary.com/Articles/kazin/alfredblake.asp>

Kleist, Heinrich von. "On the Marionette Theatre." Trans. Idris Parry, 1978. In *Hand to Mouth and Other Essays*, by Idris Parry. Manchester: Carcanet, 1981.

Nuttall, A. B. "Everything Is Over Before It Begins," a review of Stanley Fish's *How Milton Works*. *London Review of Books*, vol. 23, no. 12 (21 June 2001).

Parsons, Wendy, and Catriona Nicholson. "Talking to Philip Pullman: An Interview." *The Lion and the Unicorn*, vol. 23, no. 1 (1999): 116–134. Baltimore: The Johns Hopkins University Press.

Select Online Resources

Interview conducted by Tanya Brown at Lexicon, a literary convention in Oxford, August 2000. <http://www.avnet.co.uk/amaranth/Critic/ivpullman.htm>

Khunrath's Amphitheatrum Sapientiae Aeternae, website hosted by the University of Wisconsin-Madison's Duveen Collection. Department of Special Collections, Memorial Library, University of Wisconsin-Madison. <http://www.library.wisc.edu/libraries/SpecialCollections/khunrath/>

The English Emblem Book Project. Penn State University Libraries. <http://emblem.libraries.psu.edu/home.htm>

The Urizen Books of William Blake. Joseph Hogan, Department of Languages and Literatures at the University of Wisconsin–Whitewater. <http://facstaff.uww.edu/hoganj/gloss.htm>

The William Blake Archive. Edited by Morris Eaves, Robert Essick, and Joseph Viscomi.

Notes

page 4   "The thing about these books":
          Robert Butler, *Darkness Illuminated: Platform Discussions on "His Dark Materials" at the National Theatre.* Philip Pullman, Nicholas Hynter, Dr. Rowan Williams, Nicholas Wright, and others in conversation with Robert Butler. (London: National Theatre with Oberon Books, 2004) pp. 29–30.

page 6   "Milton is the 'deadest' of the dead poets":
          Jeffrey Hammond, "Milton at the Bat." *Antioch Review*, vol. 57, no. 1 (Winter 1999).

page 6   (sidebar) "No sacrifice to God":
          The Tenure of Kings and Magistrates (1649, 1650). The 1909 Everyman's Library edition of Milton's selected works, published by J. M. Dent (London), was used as a textual authority for quotations.

page 7   "Of Man's first disobedience":
          Ibid.

page 8   "The poet T. S. Eliot":
          See Eliot's "Note on the Verse of John Milton," *Essays and Studies*,
          1935. Gordon Campbell, editor of the 1990 edition of the Everyman
          Library's collection of Milton, puts Eliot's comment in a larger historical
          perspective. See *Complete English Poems, of Education, Areopagitica*
          (London: Dent, 1909), p. 625.

page 10   "Reversing the moral polarities":
          Philip Pullman, "Paradise Illustrated," speech made at the opening of
          the exhibition "Paradise Lost: The Poem and Its Illustrators," at the
          Wordsworth Trust, Dove Cottage, Grasmere, England. 6 July 2004.
          Copyright © 2004 Philip Pullman. Quoted by permission of Philip
          Pullman.

page 14   "of the Devil's party without knowing it"; "a true poet":
          William Blake, *The Marriage of Heaven and Hell* (London: 1790), plate 6.

page 14   "detected unorthodox energies everywhere":
          A. B. Nuttall, "Everything Is Over Before It Begins," a review of Stanley
          Fish's *How Milton Works. London Review of Books*, vol. 23, no. 12 (21 June
          2001).

page 14   "doing consciously what Blake said Milton did":
          Philip Pullman, "Paradise Illustrated," *op. cit.*

page 15   "the power of suggesting all kinds of correspondences and echoes":
          Ibid.

page 20   "mistakenly, but firmly":
          Philip Pullman, correspondence with members of children's literature
          discussion group, 11 July 2004.

page 21   "one of the most immediately recognizable images":
          Philip Pullman, "Paradise Illustrated," *op. cit.*

page 21   "Whatever its origin":
          Philip Pullman, "Paradise Illustrated," *op. cit.*

page 21   (sidebar) "At the time, I didn't have enough clout to resist":
          Pullman's personal website, <www.philip-pullman.com>. Quoted by
          permission of Philip Pullman.

page 24   "I think it's the central myth"; "There's never been a greater version":
          Philip Pullman, "Paradise Illustrated," *op. cit.*

page 24   "is the best thing, the most important thing":
          Wendy Parsons and Catriona Nicholson, "Talking to Philip Pullman:
          An Interview." *The Lion and the Unicorn*, vol. 23 no. 1 (1999) 116–134.
          Baltimore, The Johns Hopkins University Press. Copyright © 1999 The
          Johns Hopkins University Press.

page 25   "pessimistic and defeatist":
          Ibid.

page 27   "debts":
Philip Pullman, *The Amber Spyglass* (New York: Knopf, 2000) p. 521.

page 27   "His work has always been very important to me":
From a BBC Radio 4 "webchat" (undated, possibly January 2003).
Possible online resource:
<http://www.bbc.co.uk/radio4/arts/hisdarkmaterials/pullman_webchat
.shtml>

page 27   "maintain a vision":
Pullman's personal website, <www.philip-pullman.com>. Quoted by
permission of Philip Pullman.

page 28   "All Bibles or sacred codes":
William Blake, *The Marriage of Heaven and Hell* (London: 1790) plate 4.

page 30   "It's only Adam and Eve":
The visitor in this anecdote, which is often quoted but may be
apocryphal, was Thomas Butts, a friend and patron.

page 31   "somewhat taken aback"":
From notes toward Linnell's unpublished memoir. G. E. Bentley, Blake
Records (Oxford: Clarendon Press, 1969).

page 33   "He did not believe in God":
Alfred Kazin, "An Introduction to William Blake" from *The Portable
Blake,* edited by Alfred Kazin (New York: Viking, 1946). Copyright ©
1997 Alfred Kazin. Possible online resource:
<http://www.multimedialibrary.com/Articles/kazin/alfredblake.asp>

page 33   "I have to consider myself an atheist":
"Author Pullman Finds It Impossible to Believe," Heather Lee Schroeder,
The Capitol Times, Madison, Wisconsin, 13 October 2000.
Possible online resource:
<www.madison.com/captimes/books/topic/author/641.php>

page 34   (sidebar) "Unlike many other conscious beings":
Correspondence from Philip Pullman. 12 July 2004. Quoted with
permission of Philip Pullman.

page 35   "Without Contraries [there] is no progression":
William Blake, *The Marriage of Heaven and Hell* (London: 1790). plate 3.

page 36   "With the aid of vision":
Alfred Kazin, *op. cit.*

page 36   (sidebar) "reality never presents us":
C. S. Lewis, *The Great Divorce* (New York: Macmillan, 1946). pp. vii–viii.

page 38   "Lyra's a very ordinary little girl":
Interview conducted by Tanya Brown at Lexicon, a literary convention
in Oxford, August 2000. An edited version appeared in *Locus* #479,
December 2000. Copyright © by Tanya Brown. Quoted by permission.

Possible online resource:
<http://www.avnet.co.uk/amaranth/Critic/ivpullman.htm>

page 39   "I'd never heard it used as a name":
           BBC Radio webchat, *op. cit.*

page 41   "Among the 'proper' books I loved":
           Philip Pullman's personal website,
           <www.philip-pullman.com/about_the_writing.asp>

page 41   (illustrations)
           A Hundred Million Francs, by Paul Berna, translated by John Buchanan-
           Brown. Illustrated by Richard Kennedy. (Bodley Head: London, 1957).
           (Original title: *Le Cheval Sans Tête*). Also published in English as *The
           Horse without a Head*.

page 42   "the story as a whole":
           Ibid.

page 46   "'Spectre' is a core word":
           W. H. Stevenson, ed., *William Blake: Selected Poetry* (London: Penguin,
           1988). Copyright © 1988 W. H. Stevenson.

page 46   "The Spectre functions to define":
           From the glossary within Joseph Hogan's Internet site, "The Urizen
           Books of William Blake," hosted by the Department of Languages and
           Literatures at the University of Wisconsin–Whitewater.
           <http://facstaff.uww.edu/hoganj/gloss.htm>

page 47   "My Spectre around me":
           This poem, from Blake's notebooks, appears in various forms. The
           version quoted here is from *The Oxford Book of English Mystical Verse*,
           Nicholson and Lee, eds. (1917). A more complete critical version, with a
           postscript, can be found at the Blake Archive's online version of David V.
           Erdman's *Complete Poetry and Prose of William Blake*.

page 49   (sidebar) "hath borne me on his back a thousand times":
           Hamlet, Act V, scene i.

page 50   "Kleist . . . says in three or four pages":
           Kerry Fried, "Darkness Visible: An Interview with Philip Pullman,"
           Amazon.com. <www.amazon.com>

page 50   "Thrusts and feints followed thick and fast":
           Heinrich von Kleist, "On the Marionette Theatre." Translated by
           Idris Parry, 1978. In *Hand to Mouth and Other Essays*, by Idris Parry.
           Manchester: Carcanet, 1981.

page 51   "Grace appears most purely":
           Ibid.

page 52   "[I]f I am aware of myself":
           Parry, *Ibid.*

page 52   "They would come to us":
Wendy Parsons and Catriona Nicholson, "Talking to Philip Pullman: An Interview," *op. cit.*

page 53   "we must eat again of the tree of knowledge":
Kleist, *op. cit.*

page 53   (sidebar) "Innocence is belief, experience is doubt":
Kazin, *op. cit.*

page 54   "in contrast to C. S. Lewis's idea":
Wendy Parsons and Catriona Nicholson, "Talking to Philip Pullman: An Interview," *op. cit.*

page 54   "Grace is a mysterious quality":
BBC Radio webchat, *op. cit.*

page 55   (sidebar) "Working toward that end should be a joyful action":
"Philip Pullman: Some Rarely Asked Questions" ["an abridged transcript of a Q&A session given by Philip Pullman to the Balliol College English society on 6th November 2002"]. Transcribed by Thea Logie. Possible online resource:
<http://urchin.earth.li/cgi-bin/twic/wiki/view.pl?page=PullmeisterRAQ>

page 58   "What I was trying to do":
Interview by Jennifer Abbots for KidsReads.com, 12 December 2001. Possible online resource:
<http://www.kidsreads.com/authors/au-pullman-philip.asp>

page 59   "I'd always say":
Correspondence from Philip Pullman. 11 July 2004. Quoted with permission of Philip Pullman.

page 59   (sidebar) "banal evil":
See Hannah Arendt, *Eichmann in Jerusalem: A Report on the Banality of Evil* (New York: Viking, 1963). The famous phrase "banality of evil" actually appears only in the subtitle of the book.

page 61   "What I would like sensible readers":
Abbot, KidsReads.com interview, *op. cit.*

page 62   "equal to the breadth of the world":
Gustav Davidson, *Dictionary of Angels: Including the Fallen Angels* (New York: Free Press, 1967). pp. 192–3.

page 62   "spirit of fire":
Ibid.

page 64   "I suppose what lay behind my idea of Lord Asriel":
Correspondence from Philip Pullman. 11 July 2004. Quoted with permission of Philip Pullman.

page 66   "Among his associates":
          Possible online resource for *The Italian* is Project Gutenberg:
          <http://www.gutenberg.org/etext/7371>

page 66   "In him inexplicably mix'd appeared":
          Possible online resource for *Lara* is Representative Poetry Online at the
          University of Toronto:
          <http://eir.library.utoronto.ca/rpo/display/poem359.html>

page 67   (sidebar) "I have a great mind to believe in Christianity":
          Quoted in *Correspondence and Table-Talk*, vol. 2, ed. by Frederic
          Wordsworth Haydon, 1876.

page 68   "It's the theme of the rebellion against authority":
          Correspondence from Philip Pullman. 11 July 2004. Quoted with
          permission of Philip Pullman.

page 68   "paradigm":
          Ibid.

page 68   (sidebar) "one of the chief angels of destruction":
          Davidson, *op. cit.*, p. 65.

page 69   (sidebar) "was appointed to separate body from soul":
          Ibid.

page 70   "The temptation . . . is wholly beneficent":
          "Heat and Dust," an interview by Huw Spanner for *Third Way*. 13
          February 2002. Possible online resource:
          <http://www.thirdway.org.uk/past/showpage.asp?page=3949#top>

page 71   "it is interesting that in Pullman's novel":
          From a letter to *The Horn Book Magazine*, November/December 2002.
          Quoted by permission of Kristin Cashore.

page 72   "Prometheus is, in my judgement":
          Possible online resource for *Prometheus Unbound*:
          <http://www.gutenberg.org/etext/4797>

page 73   "Unable to bring mankind back to primitive innocence":
          "Prometheus: Unbound," in *The Complete Poetical Works of Percy
          Byssche Shelley*. George Edward Woodberry, ed. (Cambridge, Mass.: The
          Riverside Press, 1901).

page 75   "Mrs. Coulter surprised me by turning out the way she did":
          Fried, "Darkness Visible," *op. cit.*

page 75   (sidebar) Marlene Dietrich:
          Robert Butler, *The Art of Darkness: Staging the Philip Pullman Trilogy*
          (London: National Theatre with Oberon Books, 2003). p. 48.

page 76   "Although I felt that her attitude was changing":
          Fried, "Darkness Visible," *op. cit.*

page 76   "Dealing with her":
          Philip Pullman, correspondence with members of children's literature
          discussion group, 31 March 2002. Quoted with permission of Philip
          Pullman.

page 76   "In the nine years I have known her":
          Ibid.

page 76   (sidebar) "I was (and remain) very fond of Mrs. Coulter":
          "*Guardian* online Q&A with Philip Pullman," *The Guardian*, London,
          18 February 2002. Possible online resource:
          <http://www.guardian.co.uk/Archive/Article/0,4273,4358299,00.html>

page 77   "I think one of the things that might bother us":
          Karen S. Coats, correspondence with members of children's literature
          discussion group, 27 November 2000.

page 77   "She leapt towards what happened":
          Philip Pullman, correspondence with members of children's literature
          discussion group, 31 March 2002. Quoted with permission of Philip
          Pullman.

page 77   (sidebar) "Mrs. Coulter can be perceived as ambiguous":
          Robert Butler, *The Art of Darkness, op. cit.*

page 78   "sinister monkey":
          Correspondence from Philip Pullman. 30 June 2004. Quoted with
          permission of Philip Pullman.

page 79: (photo)
          Photo copyright © 2004 by Ivan Kyncl. Reprinted by permission of
          Alena Kyncl.

page 80   "Green Tea":
          Possible online resource for "Green Tea":
          <http://www.english.upenn.edu/~nauerbac/tea.html>

page 80   "I descended driving":
          William Blake, *The Marriage of Heaven and Hell*, plate 20.

page 80   "Yes, I know that passage":
          Correspondence from Philip Pullman. 30 June 2004. Quoted with
          permission of Philip Pullman.

page 81   "It was a silly name":
          Ibid.

page 81   "The golden monkey doesn't have a name":
          Online discussion at Readerville.com, 5 February 2001–9 February 2001.
          Possible online resource: <http://www.readerville.com>

page 81   "I didn't try very hard!":
          Correspondence from Philip Pullman. 30 June 2004. Quoted with
          permission of Philip Pullman.

page 82   "As far as I know":
Correspondence from Philip Pullman. 14 July 2004. Quoted with
permission of Philip Pullman.

page 82   (sidebar) Dave Weich interview.
Possible online resource:
<http://www.powells.com/authors/pullman.html>

page 83   "If it's lifelike at all":
Correspondence from Philip Pullman. 14 July 2004. Quoted with
permission of Philip Pullman.

page 83   "She [Mrs. Coulter] says her love came to her":
Karen S. Coats, *op. cit.*

page 87   "As Christianity grew within":
Possible online resource:
<http://www.newadvent.org/cathen/06592a.htm>

page 89   "last of all":
Plato, *Republic*, translated by Benjamin Jowett (New York, P. F. Collier &
Son, 1901)

page 90   "And now I will describe in a figure":
Plato, *op. cit.*

page 90   "It's all in Plato, all in Plato":
C. S. Lewis, *The Last Battle* (New York: Macmillan, 1956).

page 93   "a variety of the Gnostic myth":
Philip Pullman, "Writing Fantasy Realistically," a speech to the Sea of
Faith conference, 2002. Copyright © 2002 by Philip Pullman. Quoted
with permission of Philip Pullman. Possible online resource:
<http://www.sofn.org.uk/Conferences/pullman2002.htm>

page 95   "a fascinating and very powerful and persuasive system"; "The essence of
Gnosticism":
Ibid.

page 95   (sidebar) "There is only one thing worse than pain":
David Lindsay, "Sketch Notes for a New System of Philosophy," in
the University of Nebraska edition of *Voyage to Arcturus* (Bison Books:
Lincoln, 2002). Quoted in Andy Sawyer, "*A Voyage to Arcturus* by David
Lindsay" (book review), The Alien Online website, 29 October 2002.
<www.thealientonline.net.>

page 97   "the goddess of writers was smiling on Philip Pullman":
Michael Chabon, "Dust & Daemons," *New York Review of Books,* vol. 51,
no. 5, March 25, 2004.

page 97   "the old idea of the guardian angel":
Interview with Achuka.co.uk.
Possible online resource:
<http://www.achuka.co.uk/ppint.htm>

page 98   "I found it a very fruitful metaphor":
"*Guardian* online Q&A with Philip Pullman," *The Guardian*, London,
18 February 2002. Possible online resource:
<http://www.guardian.co.uk/Archive/Article/0,4273,4358299,00.html>

page 98   "the daemon is the part of you":
Pullman's personal website, <www.philip-pullman.com>. Quoted by
permission of Philip Pullman.

page 98   "The Norsemen believed ":
Sabine Baring-Gould, *A Book of Folk-Lore* (London: Collins, 1913).
Possible online resource at Sacred Texts Online:
<http://www.sacred-texts.com/neu/celt/bof/bof07.htm>

page 99   "People don't always like what their daemons become":
Robert Butler, *The Art of Darkness, op. cit.*, p. 24.

page 100 "The rebel angels led by Sophia":
Interview, BBC Radio 3's *Belief* program. Possible online resource:
<http://www.bbc.co.uk/religion/programmes/belief/scripts/philip_
pullman.html>

page 100 "If I had a spirit companion":
Kathleen Odean, "The Story Master," in *School Library Journal*, October
2000. p 52.

page 101 (sidebar) "A rather unusual gift":
Ibid.

page 102 "I loved that sinuous shape":
Catherine M. Andronik, "Philip Pullman: His Wonderful Materials," in
Book Report, Nov./Dec. 2001, vol. 20, issue 3.

page 103 "There's a real connection":
Ibid.

page 103 "Names like stoat":
Ibid.

page 104 "The pine marten":
Ibid.

page 104 "Much as I'd like to pretend":
Philip Pullman, correspondence with members of children's literature
discussion group, 4 July 2000.

page 106 "Well, this is something that came":
Wendy Parsons and Catriona Nicholson, "Talking to Philip Pullman: An
Interview," *op. cit.*

page 107 (sidebar) "That is a very good question":
Readerville.com, *op. cit.*

page 108 "I found that a very good way":
"Author Pullman Finds It Impossible to Believe," Heather Lee Schroeder, *The Capitol Times*, Madison, Wisconsin, 13 October 2000. Possible online resource: <www.madison.com/captimes/books/topic/author/641.php>

page 108 (sidebar) "magpie"; "trickster":
Pullman has referred to a magpie in several interviews. He seems to have mentioned the trickster very rarely and possibly only once, in Wendy Parsons and Catriona Nicholson, "Talking to Philip Pullman: An Interview," *op. cit.*

page 111 "These people knew exactly what they were doing":
"Ancient Figurines Found—From First Modern Humans?" John Roach, *National Geographic News*, 17 December 2003. Possible online resource: <http://news.nationalgeographic.com/news/2003/12/1217_031217_modernhumans.html>

page 111 "There does appear to be":
Ibid.

page 111 "the date at which human consciousness began":
This observation has been confirmed by Pullman.

page 114 "The first alethiometer":
Possible online resource: <http://www.randomhouse.com/features/pullman/alethiometer/history.html>

page 118 "the memory-theater system of symbolic images":
Ibid.

pages 119–120 (illustrations)
Khunrath's Amphitheatrum Sapientiae Aeternae, website hosted by the University of Wisconsin-Madison's Duveen Collection. Department of Special Collections, Memorial Library, University of Wisconsin-Madison. <http://www.library.wisc.edu/libraries/SpecialCollections/khunrath/>

pages 124–125, 127 (illustrations)
The English Emblem Book Project. Penn State University Libraries. <http://emblem.libraries.psu.edu/home.htm>

page 126 "make a moral point"; "it looked as though someone had":
Lexicon interview, *op. cit.*

page 129 "probably the same as everyone's":
Correspondence from Philip Pullman. 30 June 2004. Quoted with permission of Philip Pullman.

page 131 "the land of no return":
"Descent of the Goddess Ishtar into the Lower World," from M. Jastrow, *The Civilization of Babylonia and Assyria*, 1915.

Possible online resource at Sacret Texts Online:
<http://www.sacred-texts.com/ane/ishtar.htm>

page 132 "If I believed that my reply were made":
Translated by Henry Wadsworth Longfellow. Possible online resource at Project Gutenberg:
<http://www.gutenberg.org/etext/1004>

page 132 "I don't know very much about it":
Correspondence from Philip Pullman. 30 June 2004. Quoted with permission of Philip Pullman.

page 134 "I saw Blake's illustrations to Dante":
Readerville.com, *op. cit.*

page 137 "It has been very important for me":
Fried, "Darkness Visible," *op. cit.*

page 138 "As time goes on, my citizens will win":
Translated by Ian Johnston of Malaspina University-College, Nanaimo, British Columbia, Canada. Quoted with permission of Ian Johnston.
Possible online resource:
<http://www.mala.bc.ca/~johnstoi/aeschylus/aeschylus_eumenides.htm>

page 139 "Mine comes largely from classical mythology":
Readerville.com, *op. cit.*

page 139 "If I say anything now":
Correspondence from Philip Pullman. 30 June 2004. Quoted with permission of Philip Pullman.

page 139 "Peter Dickinson and I were talking":
Fried, "Darkness Visible," *op. cit.*

page 141 "I mistrust the biographical way of interpreting novels":
Correspondence from Philip Pullman. 30 June 2004. Quoted with permission of Philip Pullman.

page 144 "We can get out":
Ibid.

page 145 "There's a phrase":
Lexicon interview, *op. cit.*

page 145 "This republic is not so different from the kingdom":
David Boulton, "The Republic of Children," *The Guardian*, 5 April 2005.
<http://www.guardian.co.uk/religion/Story/0,2763,930278,00.html>

David Colbert

THE MAGICAL WORLDS OF THE LORD OF THE RINGS

☆ *What nightmare was the key to Tolkien's mythology?*
☆ *Can Gandalf really die?*
☆ *What does Tolkien like best about Frodo?*
☆ *Which monster from* The Lord of the Rings *attacked Tolkien in real life?*
☆ *Why are Tolkien's Elves tall?*

J.R.R. Tolkien's epic fantasies have enthralled readers for more than half a century. The realm of Middle-earth is one of the most fully realized worlds in literature, yet the remarkable mythology upon which Tolkien founded it is still a mystery to most readers.

From the Finnish saga *Kalevala* and the events in *Beowulf* to Arthurian mythology, Shakespeare, and even World War II, this indispensable guide provides insights not only into literature's most beloved fantasy, but also into the man who brought it to life.

0-425-18771-3

Available in paperback wherever books are sold, or at
penguin.com

David Colbert

THE MAGICAL WORLDS OF HARRY POTTER

"A glorious tribute to Rowling's work."
—The Times (London)

☆ *What was the model for The Order of the Phoenix?*
☆ *Where do those names come from?*
☆ *What is the real-life legend behind*
Voldemort's Dark Mark?
☆ *Could Snape's potions actually work?*

Discover the astonshing origins of supernatural beasts,
clues to hidden meanings in names, and amazing facts
about real-life wizards and magic spells. From alchemists
to unicorns, basilisks to veela, this fascinating
compendium brings another dimension
to Harry's adventures—from *The Sorceror's Stone* to
The Order of the Phoenix.

0-425-19891-X

Available in paperback wherever books are sold, or at
penguin.com